INFECTION Z 2

RYAN CASEY

Higher Bank Books

If you want to be notified when Ryan Casey's next novel is released and receive an exclusive free book from his Dead Days post apocalyptic series, please sign up to his mailing list.

http://ryancaseybooks.com/fanclub

Your email address will never be shared and you can unsubscribe at any time.

INFECTION Z: 2

ONE

Charlie Harrison dragged the heavy shopping trolley of water bottles along the potholed road and prayed today wouldn't be the day *they* finally caught up with him.

Charity Lane hadn't always been such a dumping ground. Not until the dead rose, and then the missiles struck. It was one of suburban Manchester's nicer roads, for sure. Tall, evergreen trees at either side of the smoothly tarmacked pavements. The sound of birds whistling and singing overhead. The distant chatter of a friendly little row of cafes and shops constantly in the distance.

But all that had gone.

The trees lay across the road like they'd been put there intentionally as barriers or blockades. The pavement was a nightmare to walk along, let alone pull a trolley of water bottles along, with large chunks of it unearthed. One wrong step and you'd wander right into a hole the length of your leg, sprain or break your ankle.

And you didn't want that.

Not with the dead around.

Charlie swallowed. His throat was dry. He was desperate for a drink, but he was even more desperate to get the water bottles back to Sammy and his two kids, Renate and Sebastian. Their survival was ultimately more important than his. Which was why he found himself alone in the streets in the first place, scavenging whatever supplies he could.

Because if the dead didn't raid one of the last remaining shops, other people would.

And Charlie was fast discovering that other people were just as much of a worry as the hungry dead in this harsh new world.

He listened to the trolley's wheels scrape along the pavement. The noise echoed against the shutters of the betting shops, the bookstores, on either side. He tried not to look at these stores. Tried to stay blissfully naive about what might be inside them. But every now and then, he found himself peeking through a smashed window, seeing the blood all over the white tiles of the floors, and wishing he'd not even come on this damned suicide mission at all.

He looked ahead and saw the six storey, brown-bricked flat block ahead. He was nearly home. Nearly back to his family. Which made every ounce of risk worth it. Because if you weren't willing to risk a thing for the vulnerable ones you cared for, then what was the point even having a family at all?

He heard a crow caw somewhere overhead in the grey sky. Although it had been a week since the bombs landed on Manchester, there was still a smell of cool smoke in the air, like the remains of a forest fire days after it'd gone out. Charlie knew what that smell was like because Sammy and him had been caught up in one when they'd visited California back in 2002. Delayed their holiday a few months when it clashed with a friend's wedding, then ended up getting caught in the frigging McNally Fire in the stifling heat of summer. Charlie remembered looking over the Inyo National Forest and tasting the burned pines in the air. And this brought that memory flashing back into his mind.

Except it wasn't burned pines he tasted and smelled in the air right now. It was barbecued meat.

Human meat.

He pulled on the heavy trolley filled with water bottles. His palms were sweating, and his fingers felt like they were going to pop out of their sockets. He staggered over the holes in the concrete. Just a few hundred yards from the flats his family were holed up in now. Shit. He'd expected to go out and find about five or six half-drank bottles lying around. But he'd found a whole store's worth, packed with thirty unopened bottles. Enough to last them days. Weeks, even.

A part of Charlie hoped that events would resolve themselves in the first days. That no matter how bad events got, the government would step in. And if they didn't, another country's government would step in. They always did, right?

But as Charlie looked at the devastation on the street—the smashed windows of abandoned cars, the splattering of blood on the concrete reminding him of the horrible screams he'd heard when the dead first started walking—he knew nobody was coming for him. Nobody was coming to save him or his family.

He had to look after his family himself. Provide for them. Handle things as they came. And that wasn't easy when you had two seven-year-old twins who didn't know why the hell they weren't allowed to go to school—which they loved, gracefully—all of a sudden. Or why they couldn't go round to their friends' houses for tea, or why they weren't allowed to go play on the street no matter how much Sammy and Charlie used to let them cycle along the pavement.

Life had changed. It had changed for everyone. And as far as Charlie could see, it was going to keep on changing.

He just dreaded to imagine how much it might change.

And what that change might involve.

He picked up his pace as he approached the block of flats. He was so close he could see the window of his apartment block now. The shutter blinds were closed. And no, he wasn't looking forward to locking himself away in that sweaty, dingy apartment with just the one bedroom and not a fragment of privacy. But life wasn't about the luxuries anymore. It was about sticking together.

And who knows? If they stuck together long enough, maybe they'd be able to look for an upgrade. A new place to live.

The model home that Sammy had always dreamed of but that Charlie's job in the lower echelons of the council had never been able to provide.

He stared up at the window. Sometimes, when he came out to collect food or water or any kind of supplies, Sebastian or Renate would peek through the blinds and smile and wave at their dad. And although Charlie told them not to do it because it risked attracting the attention of other not-so-living things out here in the streets, he had to admit he liked that greeting. Loved it, in fact.

It was a reminder that he was home. He'd survived another day. All was well.

He reached the crossing in the debris-laden road and he stopped when he heard movement to his right.

Hearing any sort of movement triggered an instant reaction since the dead started walking. Like a reflex muscle, one that had always been there since the dangerous days of our ancestors, but one that had nullified as the dangers of everyday life minimised.

A reflex muscle that had reactivated in full force.

He looked down the street. He couldn't see anything out of the ordinary. The usual: abandoned cars, smashed glass covering the chewed-up concrete. The occasional charred remains of a fallen tree, an electricity pylon. A body.

He took in a deep breath of the smoky air and carried on dragging the trolley across the road. He knew he was probably just being paranoid. Truth be told, this area had proven a decent place to hide out when it came to avoiding both the dead and other people. Yes, he did wake at night to the awful sound of their cold, rotting corpses dragging their feet along the road, and he did suffer intense nightmares where he was running away from them, but not just any of them—running away from his wife, his two children, who always caught up with him and tore him apart ...

An echoing noise from behind him. Like an empty Coke can hitting the road.

He swung around. Stared back in the direction he'd come from. Although it was freezing, he could taste sweat from his wrinkly, unshaven face. Nothing there. Just the wind. Just the...

He turned back around and he saw something in the corner of his eye.

It was down the road where he swore he'd heard the first noise. Just a small movement that he couldn't make out initially.

But something coming towards him.

Something moving ... fast.

He started to drag the trolley of water bottles along when he froze.

He saw the movement getting closer, and to his short-sighted eyes, it started to make more sense. And yet ... it was impossible. It had to be impossible. He'd never seen them in that kind of number before. They usually travelled in groups, but not groups *that* big.

He gripped tighter hold of the water bottle trolley and jogged across the street. In the apartment block, he could see the blinds twitching as one of his children looked out at him.

He could hear the footsteps getting closer. He had to get to his family. He had to hide. He had to get the heavy load of water inside and he had to keep quiet. Because this was unlike anything else. This was on a whole new level. This was ...

He heard the footsteps from behind.

And then from ahead.

He held his breath. Kept on holding on to the trolley handle with his sweaty hand.

This couldn't be real. This had to be a nightmare. He had to be dreaming.

He turned around.

Masses of dead unlike any he'd ever seen were piling down the street in his direction.

Just like they were from the right.

And from up ahead.

Running, and getting closer by the second.

He swallowed a lump in his throat. Felt a warm tear roll down his cheek.

He looked up at the window of the flat he was staying in. Saw Sebastian wave at him.

He lifted a hand and waved back, and then he closed his eyes when he saw Sebastian's little brown eyes widen at the oncoming mass of the dead.

"I'm sorry," Charlie muttered, as the footsteps and the gasps got closer, as the rotting smell overwhelmed his senses. "I'm so sorry."

Sammy didn't see her husband get torn to shreds by the zombies outside.

But she'd never forget her son's scream as he watched every second of his father being ripped apart.

TWO

Hayden McCall looked at the crowd of zombies gathered around the green metal fences of the abandoned bunker and felt a familiar sense of deflation.

Sarah stood beside him. They were peeking out of a metal grated opening that looked right out beyond the parking area of the bunker and at the fences. Hayden could see his breath, feel his teeth chattering, but that was just a feeling he'd got used to now. In the week since the rise of the dead, it was a rarity if he *wasn't* shivering.

"This is exactly why we can't just rely on this place," Sarah said. She was wearing a navy blue coat and blue jeans, with muddy brown walking boots on her feet. Her dark hair was tied back behind her head. It was greasy and shiny, but that was just a normality of a life without fresh water to shower or bathe in. There was a constant smell of sweat in the air. Sweat, urine, shit.

And rot. The decomposition process had well and truly set in on the zombies now.

"How many do you count?" Hayden asked, as he stared across the parking area at the zombies pressed up to the fence. He could hear the metal creaking under their weight, but the fences were strong enough to keep them out. And that's why finding this bunker in the hills just outside of Smileston and Preston was an absolute godsend.

Sarah puffed out her lips. "Six. Seven. Six or seven too many."

"We can handle six or seven," Hayden said. "We've handled more. Are you gonna give me a hand?"

Sarah sighed. "It might be six or seven now, but what about when six or seven becomes sixty or seventy? What about then?"

Hayden turned around and looked into the darkness of the bunker. He held his breath. "We cross that bridge when we come to it. For now, all we can do is take every situation as it comes."

He grabbed the sharp steel pipe that he used to pierce the heads of the zombies pressed up against the fences and stepped to the green door.

"I know you care about Clarice. She's your sister. So you're bound to be protective of her. I ... I get that, I really do. But we're freezing here. We're freezing and we're starving. There has to be some place better than here. And if there isn't some place better than here, then ... then I don't know what. But we can't give up hope on there being other places to stay. Other places to live. We can't rule that out."

Hayden pondered Sarah's words. She was right about his sister. He did want to keep her safe. After losing his mum and dad on the first day of the outbreak—or rather, *killing* his mum and dad on the first day of the outbreak—the will and urge to protect his sister had grown even stronger. He couldn't lose her. He couldn't fail her. And right now, the bunker they'd found five days ago was the safest place they had. Safer than the cold treacherous outside, that was for sure.

Hayden turned back around and looked at Sarah. "You're right. I am protective of my sister. But that's not the only reason we're staying here. We're staying here because we don't have a choice. Sure, there might be something better out there over the hills and whatever. But we don't know that. For all we know, this place could be the best place there is now. And we can't just let it go on the off chance there might be something better. I ... I'm not willing to do that."

Sarah opened her mouth to object. Then, she closed it again, looked to her feet and sighed. The gasps from the zombies gathered around the fences got louder, loud enough to send a person insane through fear if they weren't dealt with fast.

"Are you going to help me clear the fences?" Hayden asked. "Because regardless of whether we do eventually move on from here or not, I dunno about you but I'm not so happy having a bunch of those things pressed up against the railings. Their gasping, it'll only alert others."

Sarah didn't say anything. She just nodded, walked up to Hayden and grabbed a sharpened pipe much like the one he had in his hand, only this one was a little smaller. The pair of them walked to the door and yanked it open, the metal screeching against the dusty white tiles as they pulled it back.

The cold was understandably much more intense outside. It nipped at Hayden's itchy, unshaven cheeks, bit away at his protruding kneecaps. The thermal socks he'd fished out in an abandoned house just outside of Smileston on the first day following the infection had gone damp and soggy, but they were better than nothing. It was in times like these that you really came to appreciate just what a luxury central heating was.

Another luxury lost to the zombies.

Hayden and Sarah walked down the slippery concrete walkway towards the green fences of the bunker complex. It wasn't a huge place. The bunkers themselves were covered with grass and had little watchtowers on top of them. There was enough room for about twenty or so people to stay, but some of the bunkers weren't in as good condition as the one Hayden, Sarah, Clarice and Newbie stayed in. The damp was so bad inside that it got on Hayden's chest. Most of the graffiti-covered doors had their locks broken by urban explorers, so it wasn't the safest place in the world.

But it was safe enough. And safe enough was exactly what they had to settle for right now.

"I hope you're wrong," Sarah said, as they approached the seven zombies pressed right up against the fences. Their cold blood dripped down the metal from where they were pressing themselves. Flies buzzed around them. Specks of ice were attached to their skin, which no doubt did something to stop the decomposition—but not enough to banish the smell.

"About what?" Hayden asked. He stopped in front of a female zombie about half his height. She was mixed race, wearing a green jogging outfit. A large chunk had been bitten out of her leg that maggots and other creepy bugs gnawed at.

Sarah lifted the sharp pipe and poked it through the fence at a dark-haired man in an expensive looking black suit. He had a hole in his head. Hayden could see right through his cracked skull at the bites on his brain. But of course, it took more than just a movie bash to the head to kill these zombies. Actual neck damage was required. But it helped to have them down on the ground, paralysed or weakened in some way.

"About this place," Sarah said. She pressed the pipe into the suited man's open mouth. Pushed it right back as his teeth snapped at the metal. Cold blood sprayed out as Sarah wedged the pipe even further into the zombie's throat, twisting it when she reached the back of its throat and slamming it through its neck. The zombie shook a little, its glassy eyes rolled up into the back of its head, and its body went limp and slid further onto the end of the metal pipe.

"Wow," Hayden said, as he pointed right at the throat of the woman in jogging gear and slammed the sharp end of the pipe into her flesh like a snooker player potting black. "You're getting good at this."

Sarah put her boot on the fence and pulled the pipe away. The suited zombie slid away and fell to its knees, crouched with its head on the fence, blood trickling out of its wound. "See you're still getting to grips."

Hayden looked at the jogger zombie he'd pierced the neck of. He'd felt the pipe hit something solid, but not hard enough to kill the zombie. It was still moving about, every throaty gasp sending more blood dribbling down its pierced neck. He'd have to try for the neck again—any damage to the neck seemed to be enough to kill the undead, and breaking it was foolproof.

He pulled the pipe away and aimed for the neck again as Sarah moved on to another zombie—a man with ginger hair in his mid-twenties, probably about the same age as Hayden. "Stabbing somebody in the mouth doesn't come quite so easily to me."

Sarah half-smiled as the winter sun shone down on both of them. "Let's just feel fortunate we only have seven of them to deal with. Better hope it comes really easily to you when there's twice that amount."

She kept her half-smile, but Hayden could hear the sincerity in her words.

He moved on to the next zombie, a balding man wearing a blood-soaked cream fleece, lined up the pipe at the front of its mouth and slid it into its throat.

He didn't want to even think about the possibility of a larger number of zombies descending on the fences.

He couldn't allow himself to consider a threat that might take Clarice away from him.

Everything was okay. Everything was manageable.

He ignored the niggling counter voice whispering, "Sure, it's okay ... for now," in his ear.

THREE

Hayden opened the rucksack and stared at the remaining food supplies.

The four survivors all sat in the darkness of the bunker in the middle of the complex. The door was iffy and rattled on its creaky hinges in the night, but the fences were enough to keep the zombies at bay until morning. In the first few days, they'd rotated sleeping shifts with somebody on watch at all times, but there had been no need so they all just slept through the night now.

Well. They didn't exactly sleep. At least, Hayden didn't sleep. Not with the constant overwhelming knowledge that something was outside the fences of the bunker. Not with the occasional begging screams of people in the distance who were trying to get away from the zombies.

Not from the footsteps, the gasps, the groans.

"What's on the menu tonight, chef?" Newbie asked. He was wearing a long black coat and a grey wooly hat. He rubbed his hands in front of him, every breath clouding in the glow of the dim torchlight in the middle of the bunker.

Hayden swallowed a sickly taste and pulled out two packets of beef Monster Munch. "Just ... just Monster Munch."

"A packet each?" Sarah asked. She grabbed one of the packets from Hayden. "That'll do me. For an hour. Maybe an hour and a half if I'm lucky."

"Between us," Hayden said, as Sarah opened the packet. "Just ... just the two packets between us."

Sarah stopped herself reaching into the bag and looked down at the crisps like a kid being forced to share out the last slices of his birthday cake.

"Knew it was too good to be true," Clarice said. "Can't remember the last time I actually ate a proper meal."

"It'd help if you weren't vegetarian," Newbie said. He lowered his gaze and blew barely warm air onto his hands. "Just saying."

Clarice shook her head. She had short, dark hair. A camouflage jacket hung on her skinny frame. She was wearing grey jogging bottoms underneath, with a bit of skin exposed before the white trainers on her feet. Hayden figured his younger sister must be freezing, but she seemed to be coping with the cold okay. Better than any of them, in fact. "Like me being a vegetarian makes any kind of difference. How many rabbits is it you've caught since we got here?"

"Two," Newbie said, a glimmer of pride in his voice.

Clarice nodded. "Two. Two small rabbits in a week. One of them so skinny there was barely any meat on it. The other undercooked. So don't crucify me if I choose to stay vegetarian for the time being."

She reached into the bag of Monster Munch that Sarah held out for her and took a solitary crisp.

The four of them sat and ate slowly. They savoured every single crunch, knowingly or unknowingly. As if by eating slower, they'd absorb more nutrients from the crisps. Nutrients from half a bag of Monster Munch each. Who were they kidding?

"It'd help if Walkers weren't such dicks about how many crisps they stuff in a bag," Sarah said. "Only give you half a bag in the first place. So we're actually eating quarter of a bag each. A quarter of a bag of stale beef Monster Munch for breakfast, lunch and dinner. How the hell did our lives get so shitty?"

Hayden let Clarice have the bulk of his portion of crisps. His body was hungry, and he could feel his jeans getting baggier around the knees, the bones of his face sticking out more, but he just never had an appetite these days. Perhaps something to do with the things he'd seen. The zombies tearing other people apart, spilling their guts onto the ground, stuffing their faces with fresh human buffet.

Or the things he'd done. Putting down his dad's undead corpse. Holding the pillow over his live mum's face and waiting for her heart to stop ...

Actions that he lived with alone. Because he couldn't burden anyone else with the knowledge of what he'd done, especially not his twenty-year-old sister.

"We'll go out into the woods tomorrow," Newbie said, as half a crisp shook in his quivery fingers. "It's not easy hunting without proper equipment, but we'll check the traps and we'll find something. We have to find something. Failing that, we head into one of the local villages. See what we can find lying around. And failing that, we ..."

He stopped. Hayden knew what he was going to say. *We move on.* But they'd argued about moving on already. All of them had their own opinions on this bunker, and the next step. All of them agreed that this place was a good temporary shelter. As good as they were going to find, perhaps.

But it was the "perhaps" that split opinion.

Hayden and Newbie weren't too keen on taking a risk for a "perhaps."

Clarice and Sarah seemed more open to the idea of leaving this place and finding somewhere else.

"Any luck with the radio today?" Sarah asked Newbie.

Newbie shook his head. "Nothing but static. Fences all clear?"

Sarah told Newbie about the zombies at the fences. The radio Sarah referred to was an old comms room in one of the three bunkers. It had a load of old radio equipment in there, and Newbie seemed convinced that he could maybe send out a signal or receive a transmission. And Hayden got that. If they found a transmission directing them to a certain safe place, then maybe they'd have to investigate.

But he couldn't rid himself of the memories of what had happened the last time they'd gone seeking a safe place.

The military dressed in black.

Pointing their guns at Frank and blasting him to pieces.

Hunting people of all ages down.

"You okay, bro?"

Clarice's voice shifted Hayden out of his thoughts. He looked into her blue eyes and smiled. "Yeah. I ... As good as I can be."

She grabbed his hand with her icy fingers. "We'll find something. Even if it's somewhere else—"

"This place is good enough."

Clarice shook her head. "I know you're worried. Worried about me. And I'm worried about you too. But if we have to move on, we have to move on. I can look after myself."

"You won't have to look after yourself."

"I managed it for years when you ..."

She stopped. Her pale cheeks blushed. Hayden knew what she was going to say. He'd been close to his younger sister when they were in their teens. Hayden had supported Clarice in the aftermath of Annabelle—their older sister's—suicide.

But then he'd moved away to uni. And after that he'd grown even more distant. His sister's problems weren't his problems anymore. He'd let her go off the rails with drugs and booze and guys and girls. He'd left her for Mum and Dad to sort out.

He'd heard her crying out and he'd ignored her. Right up until the day he'd saved her life a week ago.

"I'm sorry," Clarice said. "I didn't mean—"

"It's okay," Hayden said. He squeezed his sister's hand tighter. "I'm here now. And I'm not going anywhere. And I won't let anything happen to you. I promise you that."

She looked at him with narrowed eyes. "You shouldn't make promises you're not sure you can keep. You've made that mistake way too many times in your life already."

Hayden looked away from his sister and leaned back on the cold tiles of the damp bunker floor. He listened to the distant groans of zombies walking around outside. Further into the distance, he could hear something that sounded like shouting, screaming. More meat for the zombies to consume. Another innocent person for them to convert to their army of masses.

"I'm keeping this promise," he said.

He closed his eyes and tried to clear his mind of thoughts.

The door at the side of the bunker creaked in the cool breeze, and the sounds of the undead armies intensified.

FOUR

ayden knew they were coming the second he heard the tapping against the front door.

His body froze. He was sat on the sofa back at his parents' house, only it was cold and uninviting unlike the plush leather delight they usually had. A part of Hayden knew it was daytime, and yet beyond the curtains, it looked dark.

But he saw their silhouettes.

Saw them clawing their long, undead nails against the windows.

Scratching their way inside ...

Hayden dragged himself to his feet but his movement was sluggish. He tried to walk across the carpet but it felt like he was wading in water—and when he looked to his feet he realised he was wading in something, only it wasn't water but blood, thick red blood getting deeper and deeper and deeper ...

He got to the bottom of the stairs. His heart raced. He knew his parents were up at the top, he knew his sister was up there, but the stairs seemed to be stretching out in front of him, the climb looked so far, and all the time the scratches were getting louder, stronger ...

He ran up the steps as fast as he could, but it wasn't fast enough. He could hear screaming. Shouting. Crying.

"Hayden, please. Please help us. Please."

His mum's voice. Or his dad's, or his sister's.

All of them, together, in pain.

He reached the top step and he looked at the door where the screaming was coming from. His body froze. Annabelle's old bedroom. But he couldn't go in there. He couldn't go in his dead sister's room. The voice inside him told him not to do that, not to go in there, to stay away.

Something bad was behind that door.

Everything bad was behind that door.

A smash downstairs. Sounds of gargling, gasping, groaning, unmistakable. So many of them, all clawing their way up the stairs, their footsteps getting louder, heavier.

Hayden didn't want to turn back and look at them. He couldn't accept they were real.

But he didn't want to go in his sister's old bedroom either.

Blood dribbled down the front of it.

Come On In Hayden Help Us Hayden Help Us Help Us Help Us ...

He had to go inside.

Dead getting closer.

Clawing out for him ...

He grabbed the handle and pulled the door open.

At first, he didn't see a thing. He just smelled it. The sour smell of damp death in the darkness.

But then he saw it.

Saw *them*.

His mum. His dad. His younger sister.

And Annabelle.

Annabelle with a belt wrapped around her neck.

Annabelle with her forearm to her mouth, teeth wedged into it, thick blood and green vomit pooling to the floor as she tore the flesh from the bone, her face getting paler and paler.

Hayden wanted to stop her. Tell her to stop. Tell her to stop hurting herself.

But then she lifted her head. Smiled at him, specks of blood in her gleaming blonde hair. She laughed at the top of her voice, and then Mum and Dad and Clarice all joined in too and Hayden saw they were bitten, the footsteps getting closer behind him, the zombies of his family all laughing as they swarmed him, sunk their teeth into him, and he screamed.

"Woah. Hayden. Cool it, man. Cool it. You're alright."

Hayden looked around the dark room. His heart was racing. Sweat poured down his head. His throat was sore, presumably from screaming out. His teeth felt smooth, like they always did when he'd ground them in the night.

"You're okay. Just dreaming. Which means you were asleep. Counts for something, right?"

Hayden lifted himself up as Newbie crouched over him. He put his freezing cold hands to his face. The door of the bunker rattled in the wind. Further in the distance outside, he could hear struggling and slicing—the sound of Sarah and Clarice dealing with the zombies stacked up to the fences.

"How long ... how long was I—"

"I only just came in here," Newbie said. "You were thrashing about like hell. But it's good you're awake. Got something to show you. Something I need you to hear before anyone else."

Hayden frowned. His head was still under the clouds of sleep as he rubbed at the icy-cold corners of his eyes. "What ..."

"Come on," Newbie said. He held out a hand to Hayden. Hayden pulled himself up in the end, but appreciated Newbie's gesture.

Hayden followed Newbie out of the main bunker and through the narrow little passageway that led through to the radio comms room that Newbie was spending a lot of time in. The old military bunker, evidently abandoned many years ago, was lined with rusty old pipes. Somewhere in the mass of pipes,

Hayden could hear the tapping of falling water, the scuttling of rats.

"Whatever you've got better be worth waking me up for. First wink of decent sleep I've got since we arrived at this place."

Newbie opened the metal door at the end of the dark corridor. "Yeah. And you looked like you were really enjoying that sleep. After you."

Hayden stepped past Newbie and went into the small radio room. It wasn't much impressive, not like the comms rooms you see on old war movies or like that amazing hatch in *Lost.* Just a room about six by six metres with a little black stool in front of some old radio devices, none of which Hayden had any idea how to use or what they even did.

When Hayden was inside the room, Newbie walked past him and rushed over to the stool. He fumbled around on the desk in front of the radio equipment, grabbed some ancient looking headphones, went to sit on the stool, then held out a hand for Hayden to sit instead. "Sit down."

Hayden rubbed the tops of his arms. His teeth chattered together. "I ... I don't—"

"Sit down. Put these headphones on. Listen."

Hayden reluctantly walked over to the stool. He perched on the end of it, and it creaked under his light weight. Newbie stuffed the headphones over both ears, and for a moment Hayden felt like he was going to get some weird form of electric shock therapy.

And then, amidst the loud crackle of the static, he heard a voice.

It was only slight. And if you didn't concentrate, it was easy to miss completely. But it was there. It was definitely there.

"What is ... what's it saying?"

Newbie reached for one of the dials and turned up the volume, but all that did was make the white noise crackle even louder.

Hayden pulled one of the headphones away so he could just hear through one ear. "What is it?"

"It's a radio transmission," Newbie said, something close to a smile on his face.

Hayden tried to listen to the voice but he could barely make out the words. Something about a "safe haven." Something about Warrington.

"Do you hear it?" Newbie asked.

Hayden strained to listen but he was beyond hope. "I ... Not really—"

"It says there's a safe haven. Just outside Warrington. That's— that's only thirty or so miles from here. It says everyone is welcome."

Hayden wasn't sure what to make of the message. He couldn't hear it properly. Couldn't make out the words as clearly as Newbie had managed. It was all just crackle. Static. Speculative at best. "Newbie, I'm not sure this is—"

"It's a transmission. A radio transmission. I've been trying to find a transmission like this for days, and finally I've found one. Someone else out there. A safe haven. Someone else alive."

Hayden couldn't ignore the bad feeling in his gut. "How do we know it isn't military? Some kind of trap to round up those who've been exposed to the infection?"

"We don't. But we can hope. Otherwise, what's the point? If we can't have some hope, what can we have?"

Hayden still wasn't certain. He was too tired to be making any kind of decisive call. "I ... I don't know. I don't know I like it. I don't know I—"

"No. I figured you wouldn't. Part of me hoped maybe you'd ..."

Hayden heard the agitation in Newbie's voice. He could tell from the way his eyes went bloodshot that he was pissed with Hayden. That a small part of him had been expecting, hoping for, a different kind of reaction.

"I ... I just don't know," Hayden said. "I don't know who I can trust. I don't think any of us can–"

"Then we just stay put here. Stay put in the cold and the damp. Stay put with no food. Then we die."

"I thought you were with me on this place?"

Newbie looked at the radio. His eyes had gone even more bloodshot. "Yeah. Yeah, I was. I was. Until ..."

He didn't finish what he was saying.

A loud, blood-curdling scream echoed from outside.

Hayden's sister's scream.

FIVE

When he heard his sister's scream, Hayden sprinted out of the comms room and through the hallway.

His heart raced. All his mind could focus on was that cry. It sounded just like it had in his nightmare. The nightmare where Mum and Dad and Annabelle and Clarice were all there, laughing at him, all bitten, all dead.

He ran into the main bunker, slipped around on the damp floor and raced towards the ajar door. He heard another shout. A shout for help. Somewhere behind him, he could hear Newbie following. He was saying things too, but Hayden couldn't work figure the words out.

All he could focus on was his sister. Making sure she was okay.

Making sure the images of blood spurting out of her savaged neck didn't come true.

He grabbed one of the sharpened metal pipes by the door. His stomach tensed. He almost didn't want to see his sister just in case something terrible had happened.

Be there for her, Hayden. Don't fail her. She's all you've got left. The one thing you have left to protect. Don't fail her.

He ran out into the greyness of winter.

Held his breath.

Both Sarah and Clarice were beyond the fences. They were surrounded by undead. Fallen undead in the most part, but for three of them that were cornering them. Clarice's sharpened pipe had wedged into the eye of one of the undead, and Sarah was busy trying to hold off one that was coming at her.

Hayden tensed his fists around the pipe and ran down the grassy verge towards the fence opening. A million thoughts flooded his mind. Why the hell were they beyond the fences? He'd specifically told Clarice so many times that she wasn't to venture beyond the fences. Cleaning the fallen undead was Hayden and Newbie's job, and sometimes Sarah's. But not Clarice's. It was too much of a risk for her. She wasn't as strong as the others. Wasn't as adept at killing the zombies.

The risk of losing her was way too high.

"Hey!" Hayden shouted as he ran down the bottom of the grassy verge and approached the gate. "Look here! Look here!"

The zombies lifted their wobbly necks. Their glassy eyes drifted in the direction of Hayden's voice, but it wasn't enough to stop them approaching both Sarah and Clarice.

Hayden grabbed the gates and tried to pull them open but … but shit. They were still padlocked. How the hell had they got outside if the gates were still padlocked? The vent at the back of the bunker? Shit. Sneaky shits.

Hayden rattled at the padlock then realised he wasn't doing much good.

"I can get the key," Newbie said. "I—I can get the—"

"No frigging time," Hayden said. He lifted the pipe and swung it at the padlock as hard as he could. It wasn't the toughest of padlocks so it had to break away with enough force.

But one blow wasn't enough.

He pulled the pipe back and went to swing it at the padlock again.

Clarice tumbled over onto her back.

The zombie standing over her reached out its filthy hands, two of its fingers missing, the remnants of gnawed bone poking through the ends.

Hayden swung at the padlock.

Harder than ever.

It cracked away. Split and hit the ground.

The gate was open.

Hayden pushed it aside. Rushed out into the land beyond—the land beyond that always felt so uncharted, so unpredictable, so dangerous—and he turned to face the zombie that was standing over Clarice.

He pulled the pipe back and swung it at the back of its neck even harder than he'd cracked the padlock.

He heard a thunk as the metal connected with bone. Watched the zombie slip to its knees, its hands holding on to Clarice's thighs.

Hayden pulled the pipe back again. He wasn't in control of himself, his thoughts, his anything.

Just swinging at the zombie.

Putting it down.

Because it wasn't taking his last living family member away.

It wasn't taking the last person he loved away.

He shoved the sharp end of the pipe into the back of the zombie's neck. He split through the rotting grey flesh and pierced the muscle, which was like the insides of an under ripe orange. He kept on pressing as blood spurted out, kept on pressing and shoving the sharp end of the pipe inside until he felt bone, and then he kept on pressing until he felt the bone crack and then the zombie went still.

It landed at Clarice's feet. She shuffled away. Her grey jogging bottoms were smeared with blood. Sweat covered her face, dripped from her dark hair.

"Shit," Sarah said. Hayden noticed Newbie had helped her

take down the zombie that she was struggling with. "Thanks for the help. We could've handled them but—"

"What the actual hell were you doing out here?" Hayden shouted.

The release of the words took him by surprise. He reached down and dragged his sister up. Adrenaline coursed through his veins as he looked in her eyes, his jaw quivering, his entire body shaking. He could see the way she was looking at him with narrowed eyes, too. Narrowed, curious eyes. Eyes that looked at Hayden in a way that told him she didn't recognise him.

"It's okay," Sarah said. "We had a close call. We—"

"I told you not to come out here," Hayden shouted. "I specifically frigging told you not to leave the bunker grounds in case exactly frigging this happened."

"Hey," Clarice said. She pushed her brother back. "Don't shout in my face. I appreciate you helping me."

"Just lay off her," Newbie said.

Hayden turned and squared up to Newbie. "She's my sister. My frigging family. Don't tell me what I can and can't do."

Newbie lifted his heavy hands. Pressed them against Hayden's chest. He stared down at Hayden. "Don't. You don't want to fight here. Believe me."

Hayden backed away and turned to his sister. He stepped over the remains of the dead they'd been burning and grabbed his sister's skinny arm again. "You stay inside in future. You stay—"

"Oh piss off, Hayden."

Clarice's words surprised Hayden. He'd never heard her swear at him. They never argued, not really. They didn't even bicker much as kids, probably because they were bound together by the collective loss of their older sister.

"I'm just looking out for—"

"I don't know what frigging guilt complex you have going on inside your head, but you're right to be feeling it."

Sarah stepped up to Clarice. "Hun, leave it."

"No, I won't leave it," she said, pushing Sarah's hand away. She looked Hayden right in his eyes. "All my late teens I've had to deal with disappointment after disappointment from you, bro. I've had to go through things alone because you were too damned lazy to show up. I've had to struggle through my exams, sleep on park benches because I was too scared to go home drunk to Mum and Dad, all because I didn't have a brother there I could rely on."

"Don't you dare blame your drink and drug problems on me."

"I wouldn't dream of blaming them on you. But the fact is, you could have been there, Hay. And not just for me. You could've been there when Dad needed help retiling the kitchen. You could've been there when Mum had a seizure and needed some extra company in A&E."

"A seizure? When did she—"

"Exactly, Hayden. Exactly. So whatever guilt problems or responsibility bullshit you've got going on, don't take them out on me. I stepped out of these fences. I took that risk. That was my bad. But it's not for you to criticise like I'm some kind of disobedient child."

She turned and walked back through the gates at the front of the bunker.

Then, she stopped. Turned around. Looked at Hayden with tearful eyes. "I don't know exactly what happened in that bedroom with Mum and Dad. I don't envy what you had to do. But you stepped up. Whatever you had to do, you stepped up. But this man I'm seeing now ... I'm seeing nothing more than a coward. A controlling coward. Don't be that man, brother. Don't be that person. You've isolated enough people in your lifetime to know when to stop."

She turned and walked up the grassy verge towards the bunker.

Hayden watched her disappear, and although he'd saved her, he saw her drifting further and further away, just like everyone involved with him did eventually.

SIX

Hayden gathered the fallen bodies of the zombies and set them on fire a few hundred metres away from the bunker.

He didn't like being out here on his own. The leafless branches of the trees scraped together and made noises like groans, voices. And there was the knowledge that zombies walked these woods. They had to do to reach the bunker in the first place.

But the undead had to be burned. If they didn't burn them, there was a strong possibility their rotting bodies would harbour and pass on some nasty diseases.

And if not, it still made sense to burn the bodies because it was the only way of truly ensuring the undead stayed dead. It took neck damage to deal with them. But sometimes the neck damage was difficult. Sometimes they had to be burned away completely before truly stopping them, and even then their fingers or toes kept on twitching way after their skin and muscle had crumbled to ashes.

Hayden dropped the match on the pile of six bodies in the middle of the open area. It was far away enough from the trees that there wouldn't be much risk of a forest fire. Or shit—maybe he was just making that up as he went along. There was a lot of that, now. In a world where everyone was adapting to new ways, there was a lot of improvisation. It was working okay for them so far, but Hayden didn't want to curse their chances.

Hayden stepped back and watched as the flames pummelled out of the pile of bodies. He looked at the faces of the dead go up in smoke. If he closed his eyes, he could trick himself that the crackling and bursting of the skin were just logs on an open fire. That the smell of burning meat was nothing more than sausages and burgers at a barbecue.

But he could never fool himself for long.

He stepped further back from the bodies, all of which he'd spent the morning dragging down here away from the bunker himself. He thought about what Clarice had said to him. All that crap about him not being there for her when she really needed him. At first, he'd found it a bit unappreciative considering he'd just saved her life. But was she right? Was he only here for her now because of the guilt he felt for letting her and their parents down in the past?

No. Of course he wasn't. Of course that wasn't true.

But a part of it, just a small part of it, ignited a spark of recognition deep inside Hayden.

"Not still moping, are you?"

Hayden swung around. "Shit," he said. "You shouldn't sneak up on me like that."

Sarah smiled. She stretched some torn leather gloves over her hands and rubbed them as the fire of bodies raged in front of them. "I dunno. It's pretty funny. And fun doesn't come cheap these days."

They stood next to one another in the warmth of the fire. Hayden felt wrong just stood here. Warming himself up in the decaying, burning corpses of innocent people—people who had been living normal lives just over a week ago. Men. Women. Children. Dads. Mums. Grandparents.

"Strange, isn't it," Sarah said.

"What is?"

She rubbed her hands. "It's kind of like a twisted circle of life. From fully fleshed people to nothing but disease-ridden fuel to give the fortunate us a bit of temporary warmth. Have you spoken to Clarice?"

Sarah's question threw Hayden off. He started to turn around.

"Wait," Sarah said. "Just ... just wait. We're grown adults. We can have a civil discussion that doesn't involve adolescent foot-stomping."

Hayden felt like answering her back or mimicking her, but he didn't want to prove her right from the off.

"She cares about you. Your sister. She's very grateful you're here for her. That you're helping keep her safe."

"With no thanks to you," Hayden said.

"We went out to clear the bodies because that's what Clarice wanted to do. I wasn't sure, but she was eager to help out."

"Then why didn't you try and stop her?"

"Because it's not my duty to stop her, Hayden. And it isn't your duty to stop her either. She's a twenty-year-old adult. A grown up, just like us. And she can make her own decisions. Sounds like she's been forced into being tough for a while now, too."

"Thanks for that. Just sprinkle a little more salt in the wound on a topic you have no idea about, will you?"

"I'm not trying to tell you how to look after your own sister. I'm not telling you how to go about your lives. But I am telling you that you have to loosen your grip. Because she just wants to help. She wants to contribute. She wants to be a part of what we've got going on here instead of some ... some charity case."

Hayden covered his mouth with his sleeve as the fumes of the burning bodies got stronger. Branches of trees whistled and danced in the wind, and every few seconds, Hayden swore he saw movement beyond them. "You saw how she was. She needed saving and bailing out right away. She's ... she's not tough like you."

"None of us are tough. I remember when we first picked you up. Vividly remember the stench of piss coming from you, the tears in your eyes. And we're all the same. We're all just scared little kids who've woken up in a horrible new world without a tit to suckle on. We've just got to figure out how to crawl as comfortably as we can before it all catches up with us."

Hayden didn't want to accept Sarah's words, but he knew deep down they were right. Something else was niggling at him too. Something he couldn't keep hidden for much longer. "Newbie found ... found a transmission."

"He found a what?"

"A radio signal. Some safe haven calling all people to wander on down there. Somewhere near Warrington, so not even that far away. He ... was telling me about it just before you got attacked. But yeah. We might have somewhere."

Hayden watched as Sarah's eyebrows raised. He knew how keen she was on getting out of the confines of the bunker. He knew how eager she was to find somewhere new, somewhere safer and more adept to housing the four of them.

"What do you think about it?" she asked.

Hayden wasn't sure whether to be honest or what being honest even meant anymore. "I ... I dunno. I just don't have a good feeling. I know that won't surprise you. But I just think it seems too ... too easy. Like, everything since the undead started walking has been a struggle. And a mythical safe haven that just so happens to be thirty miles from here? It just seems iffy to me. And I can't help but keep on thinking of Frank. What the military did to him. And what the military did to the whole of Smileston and other cities, too." He raised his hands, which shook through a combination of cold and hunger. "So yeah. Call me tin hat brigade or cynical or whatever. Can't help but feel that way. Shall we head back?"

Sarah looked at him for a few moments. She didn't say a word, as Hayden walked away from the smouldering fire, coughing as the ashes of the dead tickled his chest.

"I think you're probably right, y'know," she said.

Hayden frowned. "About what?"

"About this safe place in Warrington. I think you're probably right to be cautious. I know I've made my position perfectly clear in the past but ... maybe a bit of cautiousness isn't such a bad thing after all."

"Wow," Hayden said. "Didn't expect that from you. Now just to convince Clarice and Newbie to stay put at the five-star delight that is Hotel Bun-keur."

Sarah snorted and shook her head. "You really aren't funny."

"Then why are you laughing?"

"The same reason people laugh at Alan Partridge. The key word being 'at' there."

"I'll take it," Hayden said. "Just about."

"Please just ... just lay off your sister a bit. You can't wrap her in cotton wool. The sooner you understand you aren't solely responsible for her, the better."

Hayden didn't respond to Sarah. Because he disagreed—he *did* feel solely responsible for her. And maybe it was guilt. Maybe it was some pent up long-standing feelings of inadequacy.

Whatever it was, it was going to keep Clarice from danger.

Sarah and Hayden walked back up the frosty hill towards the bunker as the pile of bodies crackled and hissed in the flames.

They didn't see *them* coming.

Not yet.

SEVEN

To Hayden's disappointment, he didn't get to stay in the "safe confines" of the bunker long before he was out in the treacherous wild again.

He walked across the grassy hill with a fresh trap in hand. It was an idea of Newbie's—an empty plastic bottle with a small bit of food inside. A little window was cut into the side of the bottle, which small animals could crawl in through but struggled to get out of.

In theory, anyway. The traps had only really been successful once, and even then they'd only managed to catch a mouse with barely enough meat on it to feed a small kid, let alone four fully grown adults.

Newbie walked beside him. They hadn't said much since their little disagreement back in the comms room was interrupted by Clarice and Sarah. Their footsteps both crunched against the frozen ground. The sun was low but there was a gradual refreshing warmth to it, a welcome change to the ice cold they'd grown used to. The trees blew in the breeze, which kept on distracting Hayden.

But there was nothing beyond them. He was just being paranoid.

Nothing they couldn't handle, or run away from at least.

"Had time to properly think about the transmission yet?" Newbie asked.

Hayden's stomach sank. He knew Newbie was always going to break the ice eventually, he was just hoping it wouldn't be when they were out checking the old traps and placing new ones. Newbie seemed calm and composed enough, but he was a former hired killer. He'd killed people before. Hayden didn't want to push his temper over the edge.

Besides, he was twice Hayden's size.

Or more.

"I ... I just think we should all sit down and discuss it," Hayden said, remembering Sarah's surprising reluctance on pursuing the source of the radio signal. "Discuss it properly, not just on a whim."

"Have you told the others?"

Hayden didn't like the way Newbie peered at him. He wanted to lie, and the old coward inside him probably would've lied. But he had to be honest. Truthful. Besides, what problem was it if he had told Sarah anyway? "Yes. I told Sarah when we were out burning the bodies. She said—"

"So you've had the chance to poison her against moving on." He nodded. Half-smiled. "Nice one."

Hayden felt his insides tighten up. "No. I just told her it as it was."

"And what did she have to say?"

Hayden looked around at the trees. Again, he swore he saw movement way in the distance, but the movement was like the floaters you got in your vision sometimes. When you weren't focusing, they were so ever-present. When you tried to focus, they slipped out of view.

"She ... she said she thought it'd be better if we all discussed it too—"

"Bullshit. Try again. What did she say?"

Hayden stepped through a slushy section of the grass as the bare trees around them got thicker. "She ... she's not sure. But hear me out—she's just worried about what happened to Frank. Worried it's some kind of trap."

Newbie brushed aside some branches scratching against his cheeks. "Hayden, when the hell will you see it? This is the trap. This is the trap that we're in right now. Living this way. Barely fucking living at all. This is the trap. This is what the military want. Don't you see that?"

Hayden was surprised by two things. One, to hear Newbie swear. He didn't seem to swear much. Probably the least of them all.

But there was something else, too.

"Why the sudden change in tune?" Hayden asked.

Newbie lowered his head. He searched the leaf-covered ground for the trap they'd placed yesterday. "I don't know what you're talking about."

"You—you were with me. With me on this bunker. On how it wasn't such a bad place. How it's secure at the very least. And now you've heard a few crackly words on a radio signal telling you to go to Warrington, you're crazy about leaving. What is it? Why the sudden change?"

At a glance, it looked like Newbie was still searching the ground. But on closer inspection, Hayden could see that Newbie wasn't really staring at anything in particular. He was shaking. Something wasn't right.

"We've known each other over a week now. We're living together until ... well, until whenever the end of this infection is. You've told us things and we've all told you things. Why are you so desperate to leave all of a sudden? What's ... what's in Warrington?"

Hayden saw something in Newbie's eyes when he looked up at him. Tears.

Tears in Newbie's eyes. Something that definitely didn't come lightly.

He leaned back and rested his arms on his knees. He stared at the frosty grass in front of him. "Seven years ago, I ... my ex-wife won custody of my kid. Amy, she was called. Only three when she went to live with her mum. And the courts, they ... they accused me of being violent. Having a nasty temper. Spreading venom and saying I mouthed off about her mum. So ... so Amy couldn't come stay at my house anymore. She couldn't visit her own damned dad's house. I ... I had to make do with contact centres or damned McDonalds trips. And I couldn't hack it. It ... it just wasn't right."

Hayden listened to the words pour out of Newbie's mouth. He got the impression they weren't words Newbie had uttered very often.

"So I gave up. I gave my own damned daughter up. Sent her birthday and Christmas money but I wonder whether her mum even gave her those. Martha could be poison when she wanted to be. But ... but shit. She'll be ten now. Nearly starting big school."

Hayden crouched beside Newbie. The ground was cold on his already cold ass. "And she's in Warrington?"

Newbie nodded just once. Tears were streaming down his cheeks. "I just ... I couldn't stop thinking about her when the infection broke out. Couldn't stop wondering and worrying and hoping and praying. And ... and then I heard the signal. I heard the signal and it gave me hope, y'know?"

He looked at Hayden now, and Hayden understood the pain behind his eyes. He'd felt that pain himself when his mum had called him and begged for help. He'd heard she was alive, and after that point, he had no choice but to try and save her.

"I didn't want to say because I don't like weighing other people down in my own emotional baggage. But now you know. I have to go to Warrington. With or without you all."

The final words hit Hayden hard. Because Newbie said them with defeat. And in truth, it was probably defeat that was well placed. There would be a reluctance to move on to Warrington on a whim. And yes, it was awful of Hayden because Newbie had followed him when he'd gone to Preston to save his family.

But things had changed. Circumstances had changed. Their understanding of the dangers of the outside world had changed.

"We'll talk about it," Hayden said. "All of us. As soon as we get back, we'll talk about it."

Hayden knew from the half-smile Newbie gave him that he understood what he was saying. The radio transmission wasn't enough to go on. It was speculative at best. Suicide at worst.

"Hold up," Hayden said. He stood up and walked over to where the trees thinned. He crouched down at the edge of the woods and lifted up the plastic bottle trap that they'd lain yesterday.

Inside, a grey squirrel was rustling around trying to escape.

Newbie smiled and walked over to Hayden. "What'd I tell you? These traps are foolproof."

Hayden looked at the squirrel, looked at the fear in its beady black eyes, and he felt sympathy for it. Survival of the fittest had multiplied since the fall of society. "Just got to be careful not to let it go—"

"Wait. What's that?"

Newbie's voice diverted Hayden's attention from the squirrel. He was squinting through the trees to the dip in the hill. Hayden looked too, and he swore he saw movement.

Only this time, the movement didn't slip from his vision when he focused on it.

Newbie and Hayden walked slowly through the thinning trees to the edge of the hill. They didn't say a word. They didn't have to. The cold wind blew stronger against the trees. The smell of the burned bodies earlier drifted into their nostrils.

They stopped at the edge of the hill.

Stared down the hill.

Hayden couldn't quite understand. He couldn't quite comprehend.

But he dropped the trap to the floor and the squirrel scrambled free.

And none of them even tried to stop it fleeing.

Not with what was ahead of them.

At the bottom of the hill.

Heading their way.

EIGHT

"We ... we need to get back to the bunker. We need to let the others know. Hayden."

Hayden heard Newbie's words. But he couldn't focus on them. He couldn't comprehend them. He was too focused on what was heading up the hill, heading towards the trees, heading towards the bunker—towards their safe haven.

"Hayden, we can't stand around here. We have to let Sarah and Clarice know. And we have to get away from here."

Hayden stepped back over the frosty grass. He kept his eyes on the things approaching. The stench of rotting was strong, the cold wind making it even more intense. The sound of them was unlike anything Hayden had heard, too. A thousand gasps, all echoing over the landscape.

He blinked. Rubbed his eyes. Tried to make sense of what was marching up the hill.

It didn't make any more sense when he saw it this time, but he understood what it meant.

The fields at the bottom of the hill were filled with undead. They were clearly undead because of the way they were staggering along, the way some of them at the front of the pack jogged up

the hill and in Hayden and Newbie's direction. There were so
many of them. More than Hayden had ever seen in one single
place.

Shit. More than Hayden had ever seen put together.

Coming for him. For his friends. For his sister, and for the
bunker.

He turned and jogged back towards the bunker. His legs were
like jelly. As he moved, he couldn't avoid the sounds of the
echoing groans drifting up the hill, drifting towards him. He
didn't know what to do. Where to go. The fences of the bunker
had to hold. They just had to lay low. Keep quiet.

The fences would hold strong.

Hayden and Newbie ran through the grass and saw the bunker
close by. Hayden just wanted to get back. Back to his sister. He
had to know she was okay. He had to be there for her. They had
to fight through this, one way or another.

Hayden was so focused on getting back to the bunker that he
didn't see the three zombies approaching through the trees on the
left until they were clutching at the sleeves of his coat.

He swung around at them. Pushed the one grasping him away
and sent it crashing into the two behind it, and then he kept on
running, kept on moving towards the bunker. It seemed like the
nightmare he had where the stairs felt like they were stretching
further above him. He was tired. Exhausted. He wasn't sure how
much further he could run, only that he had to.

He had to, because he had to get back to Clarice and Sarah.

He had to get back.

Hayden and Newbie emerged from the edge of the trees.
Hayden could see both Clarice and Sarah in the grounds in front
of the bunker, but they hadn't seen him yet. He wanted to shout,
but he knew shouting wasn't a good idea because it would only
draw the mass of zombies right to their doorstep.

He pushed the gate aside with shaking hands and noticed that
the padlock was broken from earlier. Shit. They hadn't had time

to replace it. It wouldn't hold. The doors in the bunker wouldn't hold.

Shit shit shit.

Clarice and Sarah saw Hayden and Newbie when they rushed inside the yard of the bunker. Sarah smiled, Clarice frowned. "Guys, what's—"

"We need to get out of here," Newbie said, panting. He turned and looked at the trees. So too did Hayden. No movement. No sign of the oncoming mass of zombies yet.

But they were coming.

They'd be here for them soon.

"Wait, slow down," Sarah cut in. "What's going on?"

"At the bottom of the hill," Hayden said, struggling to catch his breath. "There's ..." He tried to put what he'd seen into words. "Zombies."

"We can handle—"

"More zombies than we've ever seen," Hayden said. "I mean ... hundreds. Probably thousands. All—all together as one big group. All coming this way."

Clarice frowned. She had a bemused look on her face like she couldn't quite take her brother's words seriously. "How ... what ..."

"I don't know how, I don't know what and I don't know why. But we need to get inside the bunker. We ... we need to get inside the rear exit tunnel. We need to hide down there and wait for them to pass."

Newbie turned and frowned at Hayden. "You can't be serious."

Hayden could hear the footsteps of the oncoming zombies getting closer. "We ... we can't leave this place. We can't give it up. We have to hide."

Newbie's eyes went red. His lips quivered. "After everything we just spoke about. After everything I just told you."

"Whatever we do, we can't frigging stand around here," Sarah said. "Into the main bunker. Gather our stuff and—"

"There's no time to gather our stuff," Newbie said sharply.

"Not a moment of damned time to gather our stuff. They'll be here any second. And we don't want to be trapped in this place when they get here."

Clarice looked at Hayden, waiting for his response. Sarah wandered towards the bunker door. The smell of decaying corpses got stronger.

"Hayden," Newbie said. He stared at Hayden intensely. "You saw them. You stood beside me on the edge of that hill and you saw them. There were hundreds of them. Thousands, like you said. Don't be stupid here. We need to leave. We need to get as far away from here as possible while we still have the chance."

Hayden didn't respond to Newbie. He wanted to, but he couldn't. Because he knew deep down that Newbie was right. Holding onto this place was stupid. Reckless. Suicidal. And sure, leaving the bunker complex was all those things, but a little less so than sitting here like cattle waiting for the slaughter.

Unless they hid, and hid fast.

"Quick," Hayden said. "We need to get to the tunnel. We ... we decide what our next step is down there."

The four of them jogged to the entrance of the bunker. Hayden didn't once turn around. He didn't want to risk looking at one of the zombies, didn't want an undead corpse staring back at him. It was like playing hide and seek with his older sister as a kid. He was convinced that if he squeezed his eyes shut, he was more disguised in some way. Didn't matter if his foot was sticking out or a bit of his hair was on show, he just had to squeeze his eyes and the luck of the game would be on his side.

Only he knew now that was bullshit. That was fantasy.

Reality wasn't a game of frigging hide and seek.

They rushed inside the door of the bunker. Hayden swung around, looked at Clarice as she got closer to the door, sprinting as fast as she could. She didn't look scared, just ... bemused. Bemused, like she always did in horrible situations. Like life was one big cruel joke and she couldn't believe the ridiculousness of it.

Hayden grabbed her hand when she reached the door and pulled her inside the bunker. He pushed the metal door shut, but it wouldn't close properly, another screwed-up lock. Just what they needed right now.

He thought about sliding a table in front of it or something. Not that a desk would do much to stop the progression of a thousand zombies, but it'd give him more peace of mind.

But there wasn't any time for peace of mind.

"Hayden. *Come on*. We need to get out of here."

Hayden turned. He saw Newbie standing by the rusty grey door to the dark tunnel. He was looking at him with fear, or was it disappointment?

Or happiness at finally getting a valid enough excuse to push on to Warrington?

Hayden started to walk towards the tunnel door.

And then he saw the shadows cutting through the light on the tiles in front of him.

He held his breath. Turned around. Looked through the rectangular ventilation hatch that the group found more useful as a window.

The mass of zombies was right outside the fences.

Pressing themselves up against the metal.

The fences creaked under their mass of rotting weight, and the undead got closer to the unlocked gate, so so close ...

NINE

Hayden tried to blot the sounds of the undead groans echoing through the tunnel from his mind as he walked into the darkness.

Clarice, Newbie and Sarah walked with him. They were all holding weapons of choice—the sharpened metal pipes, as well as an individual weapon each. Newbie had an axe. Sarah had a long blade. Clarice had a wrench.

Hayden clasped his hands around the mallet and walked further into the unknown.

"So we're leaving this place," Newbie whispered, his voice echoing against the claustrophobia-inducing brick walls. "I'm guessing that much is settled right now."

"Let's just ... let's just make our way through here as quietly as we can without tearing each other's throats out," Sarah said. "We're okay for now. But we don't know how long 'for now' is gonna last."

Hayden and Clarice walked close to one another. He couldn't hold her hand because they were both carrying two weapons each. But he felt her warmth beside him. Heard her shaky breathing contrasting the grunting, the gasping, the rattling of the fences that surrounded the bunker.

He was here for Clarice. It didn't matter how weak or how strong or how *whatever* she was, he was her big brother and he was here for her. And that's what mattered.

Newbie coughed a little as they walked further into the dark pit of the tunnel. The temperature seemed to dip completely in here— which said a lot considering how damned cold it was outside. The smell of damp was strong, so strong that it made Hayden want to heave. His stomach churned with hunger, the thought of a spicy curry or spaghetti Bolognese teasing his senses, but his appetite was barely present as the taste of sweat lingered on his tongue.

"Swear I don't remember this tunnel being this long," Clarice whispered.

"That's 'cause you weren't hiding from zombies when you last came this way," Hayden said. "It ... it can have that kind of effect on a person."

But Clarice was right. The tunnel was longer than Hayden remembered it being too. In a way, that was a good thing. It meant that the zombies would have some work to do if they were to reach them.

But in another way, it was a bad thing. Because like in his nightmares, Hayden couldn't shake the feeling that no matter how far he ran, how much he tried to hide, the monsters of the dark would always catch up with him.

"If we're gonna stop, now might be a good time," Sarah said.

"We aren't stopping," Newbie said. "We get out of this tunnel while the infected are surrounding the fences. We get the hell away from this bunker complex, preferably before they find the entrance to this tunnel."

Hayden shook his head. "Newbie, *you* saw how many of those things were out there too."

"Which gives us all the more reasons to leave."

"No. It gives us all the more reasons to think about what we're going to do. Say we do leave this tunnel. What then? Run away from them in the opposite direction to Warrington? How long do you think our undernourished, dehydrating bodies are gonna carry us?"

"We loop around them," Newbie said defiantly. "We'll find a vehicle of some kind."

"Well I'm glad to hear you're confident. Really. It puts me at ease knowing there'll be a vehicle casually waiting outside the tunnel for us."

Newbie stopped and faced up to Hayden.

"Guys." Clarice put a hand between them. "We're all stuck here. We can't tear each other apart."

"That's the zombies' job," Sarah quipped. Nobody laughed.

Hayden held his gaze with Newbie. He'd come a long way in just over a week. Back in the normal world, before it all went to shit, he wouldn't have considered standing up to someone. But right now he felt it important to get his views across. For his point to be heard.

"I'm just saying we should wait until ... until we know we absolutely have to leave. If the zombies don't know we're down here, they'll just walk on."

"I know you care about keeping your sister away from the real frigging world, but I care about keeping the whole lot of us safe."

Hayden's jaw tensed. "Oh, oh really? And—and this is nothing to do with your daughter? Nothing to do with—with the daughter you failed? Leading us all into a death trap for a daughter you haven't seen since she was—"

Hayden felt a smack across his face and tasted the strong metal of blood right away. His head went dizzy, his face felt like it was swelling up. The sound of Sarah and Clarice gasping sternly at Newbie to back off rattled in his eardrum.

Hayden put a hand to his face. Felt his cheek. It was bleeding, and stung like hell.

"You don't dare make this about my daughter," Newbie said. He was trying to get at Hayden again, but Sarah and Clarice were doing an admirable job of getting in his way. "You don't make this about my Amy."

"Then you—you don't make this about me and my sister," Hayden said. Just speaking sent a horrible shooting pain right through his jaw. "You ... you don't make this about me trying to protect my family when you're only trying to do the same."

Newbie pushed Sarah aside and went at Hayden again with the metal pipe raised.

For a moment, Hayden actually thought Newbie was going to stab him, there and then. The humanity had drifted from his eyes. There was a vacancy in them that Hayden rarely saw in other people, more akin to the blank expressions of the undead.

And then Newbie stopped. Lowered the pipe. Shook his head and turned around. He walked off in the direction of the tunnel exit.

"Newbie, wait," Sarah said.

"Oh, leave him," Hayden said, waving him off, blood trickling from his face and echoing on the damp concrete floor. "Let him kill himself for all I care. Let him ..."

He felt Clarice's hand on the back of his neck.

Looked up, saw her peering at him with narrow-eyed concern.

"You okay?" she asked.

Hayden held his sister's stare. He touched the wound on his cheek with the tips of his fingers then backed away as a stinging jolt shocked his body. "I ... I'm sore. Sore, but—"

"Do you hear that?"

Newbie's voice surprised and annoyed Hayden. He stood up. Looked at him as he stood with his back to the rest of the group in the tunnel. Adrenaline coursed through Hayden's system. "All I can hear is the sound of a fucking nutcase—"

"Footsteps. Ahead. Do you hear them?"

Hayden stopped. Sarah and Clarice stood still. They listened, but all Hayden could hear was the trickling of water, the scuttling of rodents and insects, and further away behind them, the rattling of the fences and the gasps of the undead. "I don't hear anything. We should keep quiet. Stay put for now."

"Sarah, Clarice, you *did* padlock the rear entrance door when you finished clearing out the bodies this morning, didn't you?"

Sarah and Clarice looked at one another with widened eyes.

Clarice opened her mouth first. "I ... We—"

"We were about to when ... when you came running over," Sarah added. "But ... but it'll be okay. They're behind us. Right?"

It was at that split second that Hayden heard the creaking of a door somewhere in the distance right at the end of the tunnel.

It was a second later that he heard the fences crash to the ground from the opposite direction.

They stayed still. Stayed still, stunned and in silence.

Hearts pounding.

Listening and praying.

Then: footsteps echoing from the rear exit.

A throaty gasp.

Another.

"Run," Newbie said.

TEN

Hayden sprinted as fast as he could down the darkened tunnel away from the oncoming footsteps.

His heart raced. The floor was slippery and damp, so he felt he could lose his balance at any moment. He could hear the gasps of the zombies echoing their way through the rear entrance of the bunker. He didn't know how far away they were exactly, but he knew there were a lot of them.

And he knew from the frantic patter of their footsteps that they were coming for him, coming for all of them.

"We need to get the hell out of here," Newbie gasped. "No ... no time for messing around and holding onto hope anymore. This place isn't safe."

Hayden wanted to shout something at Sarah and Clarice. Wanted to lambast them for not putting the lock on the rear entrance as soon as they'd had the chance. He wanted to, but he couldn't, because he could hear the echoing groans of the hundred-strong mass of zombies getting closer as they ran into an oncoming storm.

"They ... they're at the fences," Sarah said. "They're at the fences. So how are we supposed to get past them?"

Newbie didn't answer at first. He just kept on sprinting. The footsteps behind them were getting louder, faster. The smell of rot drifted through the tunnel. "I ... I don't know. I don't know. But we have to try something."

They ran for what felt like forever before Hayden spotted the tunnel entrance door just up ahead. He felt a momentary relief, but that momentary relief was instantly quashed by the knowledge of what was on the other side.

Zombies. Lots of them.

He hoped they hadn't got through the fences. Even though he'd heard the sound of metal splitting, he had to hope they hadn't made it inside the actual bunker complex.

All of them had to hope, for their own sakes.

"There were so many of them," Clarice said. "I don't know how the hell you're expecting us to just run through them—"

"Me neither," Newbie said sternly. "But we don't have a choice. Things have changed. It's die in here versus probably die out there. I'd rather take my chances."

They sprinted further down the tunnel until the door was in touching distance. A stitch crippled Hayden's stomach, and he could taste blood from where Newbie had hit him.

He had to accept the truth now. Accept the reality of their situation. The tunnel plan had failed. There was no staying in here. Doing so was suicide.

"We could try the comms room," Hayden said. "Close the door. Stack up a few desks and stuff against it."

"And then what?" Clarice asked. "Starve to death inside while the undead settle down in the rest of the bunker?"

Clarice had a point, but Hayden didn't want to admit that to her. "I just ... I don't want to give this place up. I don't want—"

Hayden's voice was interrupted by a shout.

A deep voice behind him.

He swung around and saw Newbie was on the floor. He looked like he'd slipped on the wet ground.

And behind him, the silhouettes of the dead were approaching.

"My ... my ankle," Newbie said. He tried to stand up, but tumbled back down again.

"Shit," Sarah said. She backed away. "We—we don't have much time."

"I just need a hand," Newbie said. "Just ... please. Pull me up."

Hayden stood still. He stood and watched the dead get closer. He couldn't explain the voice inside his head that was telling him to run. Whispering in his ear that Newbie was a good distraction, a good bit of bait that would help them escape the tunnel.

"Hayden!" He felt a punch on his arm. Clarice. "Come on. He needs a hand!"

Hayden swallowed a lump in his throat and snapped the tempting thought out of his head. He wanted to run. He wanted to get out of here and away from the oncoming dead.

But he couldn't. He couldn't just give up his humanity.

He ran back to Newbie and grabbed his armpits. Newbie winced as he stood, then twisted his foot around on the ground. Hayden swore he heard a click. "Damned thing is always twisting. But ... but I'll be okay."

"Not if we don't get the hell out of here fast, you won't."

Hayden swung around and supported Newbie as they closed in on the rear exit door. He could hear the echoing cries of the undead getting closer, closing in, readying their worn down teeth to sink into their flesh.

They reached the door. Hayden could hear groaning beyond it.

"We ... we can't just wander out there," Clarice said. "There might be infected inside."

Hayden held his breath and grabbed the handle of the door. Behind him, he could hear the running group of zombies nipping at their heels. "But there's definitely dead in here. So we have to take a chance."

He lowered the handle.

Please please please.

He pulled the door open.

His eyes stung at seeing natural light again. But as Newbie, Clarice and Sarah hurried out of the tunnel, Hayden could see one positive—there were no zombies in the bunker. The main door wasn't even open.

"Close the door, Hayden!" Sarah said.

Hayden turned around. He went to swing the tunnel door shut, and then he saw them in the light.

Rotting.

Blood soaked.

Limbs and torsos pierced with bloody bite marks.

At least a dozen of them, all coming in his direction.

He slammed the door shut. Stepped away from it. He knew it was futile. They'd bang at the door and eventually they'd figure out how to lower the handle. They wouldn't give up. When all they cared about was human flesh, they wouldn't ever give up for anything.

Newbie winced as he hobbled over to the window area that looked out at the bunker grounds. Sarah and Clarice both joined him, as Hayden held back and listened to the sound of oncoming footsteps.

"Shit," Sarah said. "Holy shit."

Hayden didn't even want to see what Sarah was cursing about. He didn't want to accept his inevitable fate.

"We ... we might actually have a chance," Clarice said.

His sister's voice took Hayden by surprise. He turned and looked at the light piercing through the grey clouds and peeking through the window.

"We need to be fast," Newbie said. He winced with pain again as he applied more weight to his ankle. "And ... and I'm not sure how fast I can go."

Hayden walked to the window. Kept on holding his breath. Looked outside.

To moderate disappointment, there hadn't been some kind of cataclysmic event that wiped out every zombie in the bunker grounds. There *were* zombies in the bunker grounds. A lot of them. Tens, maybe hundreds.

But the bulk of the group were drifting to the left of the bunker. Following one another like a colony of ants, working their way around the side of the complex.

There was a gap to the left of the zombies.

A gap that led down into the woods.

A chance to make a break for it.

"I know you don't want to do this," Newbie said, looking at Hayden. "And ... and I get that. We're scared. We're all scared. This world isn't easy for any of us. But we have to leave here now. We have to leave here, and this is the only chance we're gonna get. We have to make a break. You see that now, right?"

Hayden did see that. He saw the gap between the rotting bodies. He saw a chance to sprint for his life. Or for his death. Or for whatever fate lay ahead.

He grabbed his sister's cold hand. Looked at her, his eyes welling up.

"I'm sorry for earlier," he said.

Clarice smiled shakily. She rubbed her face with her sleeve. "It's ... it's okay—"

She didn't finish what she was saying.

A crash hit the tunnel entrance and the door rattled off its hinges.

ELEVEN

The group didn't have any more time to deliberate when the tunnel door snapped off its hinges and the crowd of zombies tumbled inside the bunker.

"Quick!" Sarah shouted.

There wasn't any time to stand around. Hayden ran towards the side door of the bunker, the mallet tightly between his sweaty fingers. He yanked the door open, made sure the others got out before him.

And then he felt something scrape against his arm.

He swung around. A woman with straggly dark hair and a face covered with mud and blood. Her teeth were yellow and rotting, and she smelled unwashed—like she was a mess well before the world went to pot.

She had a raw red bite mark on her right shoulder, the skin around it turning a nasty shade of purple.

Hayden swung the mallet right in the middle of the zombie's forehead. He heard the bone crack under the immense force, felt cold blood splatter onto his hands.

And then he pulled the mallet out of her head and sprinted outside, no time to deal with her neck.

He slammed the door shut. Her wrist caught inside it. She scratched around with her long, unkempt nails, trying to hold on to something.

So Hayden swung the mallet at her hand.

Still, she kept on struggling, and the force behind the door from the other zombies grew stronger.

"There's no time," Sarah said. "Just—just run, Hayden. We need to just run."

Hayden turned and saw the dozens of undead roaming the bunker grounds start to look in their direction. The vast crowd drifting to the left of the bunker were slowing down too. He couldn't risk attracting their attention or he'd definitely be dead. Clarice would be dead. All of them would be dead.

He felt a bang against the bunker door. Another set of fingers, one of them chewed down to a bony stump, wedged into the gap.

"We need to go," Clarice said, starting to jog down the pathway. "They're right, bro."

Hayden held his breath. He pressed back against the weight of zombies behind the door. His sister was right. Everyone was right.

They had to go.

He pushed against the door as hard as he could, and then he ran.

He heard the door smack open the second he let go of it but he didn't have time to wait around. He ran after Clarice, Sarah and Newbie—who was hobbling along at half the speed he usually hit thanks to his twisted ankle. He saw the dozens of zombies drifting towards him, reaching out for him, men women and children, all hungry, all desperate for a taste of their fresh human flesh.

Hayden swung the mallet at the first of the zombies that came at him—a black man probably in his twenties around the same age as Hayden. His white shirt was split, and blood and flesh drooped from a gaping wound on his neck.

Hayden split his skull open, sent him flying to the ground, struggling and shaking to regain his footing.

Hayden kept on running. He didn't want to turn back because he could feel how close the zombies behind him were. He could hear their cries echoing around his skull. He just had to keep going. Just had to press on. Just had to get the hell out of here, get to safety, get Clarice to safety.

Wherever and whatever safety was.

A tall, skinny man wearing a black priest's outfit snarled at Hayden as he ran past, getting closer to the bunker gates. His eyes were greyed and clouded over; his front teeth were chipped and cracked.

Hayden swung at the front of his neck, slammed him square in his Adam's apple. He heard the zombie let out a choking sound, knew he'd be back on his feet again in seconds, but he didn't have the chance to finish it off.

The group were just metres away from the bunker gate now. Just metres away from getting the hell out of here. And sure—the zombies would chase them and keep on chasing them now they knew they were here. But they could go into the woods. Hide. Hide and hope.

Hayden figured a lot of hoping was going to go down if they survived this.

"Shit. They ... they're turning."

Sarah's voice caught Hayden's attention through the deafening shrieks and pounding footsteps of the zombies. She was looking over to her right at the direction the zombies were heading.

Were heading being the operative term.

The zombies at the back of the crowd were splitting off and drifting in the group's direction. They were approaching the open gate. Fast.

"Gonna have to move fast," Newbie said.

"You keep on saying that like I'm gonna just stop for a breather or something," Clarice said.

They ran down towards the gate. The dozens of zombies in the bunker grounds were all onto them now, and the ones that had chased them through the tunnel still weren't giving up.

Sarah pulled open the gate, waved Newbie and Clarice and Hayden through.

"Everyone for themselves out there," she said, looking at Hayden as he stepped out of the gate and into the terrifying unknown. "We run and if we get split up, we get split up. We survive. That's the main thing."

Hayden nodded and looked over his shoulder at the bunker grounds.

He regretted it right away.

The zombies at the front of the pack were just six metres away, and they were running.

"Sarah, you—"

"I'll let you get a head start. Newbie definitely needs one. Now hurry up and go."

Hayden frowned. The zombies were so close. So close to reaching her, so close to tearing her apart. "But you'll ... you'll—"

"I can handle my-pissing-self, alright?" she said. "Now go!"

Hayden didn't need any extra encouragement.

He turned and he ran as fast as he could in the direction of the trees, in the direction of Newbie and the direction of Clarice.

He heard the gasping drift further behind him, heard Sarah rattling at the fences, goading the zombies to come closer. He didn't know what she was doing. What she was thinking. But whatever it was seemed to be working.

He ran through the crippling aches in his knees and the dizziness in his head and the thirst and the hunger and everything.

He swung at the zombies that wandered through the trees towards him. He swung, even though his arm was exhausted, even though his body was completely and utterly spent.

He ran and ran and ran.

When he got into the middle of the woods and he hadn't

heard or seen the zombies for a while, he turned and looked back through the trees.

He couldn't see the bunker. He couldn't see the safe haven.

And he couldn't see Sarah.

He felt a hand on his arm.

"Come on," Newbie said. "We ... we need to move."

Hayden thought of asking about Sarah. Asking what they could do for her. Whether they could go back and help her. Or wait for her, at least.

But then he heard the gasps echo from the other side of the trees and he knew she was gone.

He knew that safety itself was gone.

He turned, put an arm around his sister's shoulders, and together they ran further into the unknown.

TWELVE

Hayden had no idea how long the three of them had been traipsing through the desolate woods and over the barren hills when he finally had to stop.

His legs wracked with the pain of all the running he'd done. His lungs were weak and raspy. Sweat dripped down his face and coated his entire body, but the temperature was so low that it felt like he was taking a cold water shower that he couldn't step out of. He could taste all kinds of combinations of foods he wanted—burgers, curries, chips, all sorts of fatty and greasy products—but couldn't have. Foods he hadn't been able to have since the world fell apart just over a week ago.

And now the three of them were being expected to march on to Warrington.

Clarice rested her hands on her knees as they stood at the top of a field. It wasn't particularly distinctive. The sun was low and the frosty ground was beginning to thaw out, just in time for it to freeze all over again that night. In the distance, Hayden could see a motorway filled with cars. Cars that had been abandoned long ago. Cars that would eventually rust away, that weeds would work their way around and make a part of the landscape, of the surroundings.

Cars that would rot away, just like everything did in this world, now more so than ever.

"We've been walking hours," Clarice said, panting. "We ... we need to take a breather or we'll—"

"The sooner we get to Warrington, the better," Newbie said. He kept on walking. Kept his head up. Stayed focused on the countryside ahead.

Hayden put a hand on his sister's back. "We'll find somewhere. Somewhere to stop and recharge our batteries. Somewhere maybe Sarah can—"

"Sarah isn't coming after us," Newbie said. He didn't turn around. His tone was cold. It was like he'd snapped the second he'd heard that radio transmission, like all his hopes and focus were pinned on the chance that his ten-year-old daughter that he hadn't seen for seven years might, just might, be in Warrington. "She did a selfless thing. But she isn't coming after us."

Hayden couldn't argue with Newbie's judgement. The last time he'd seen Sarah—the last time any of them had seen Sarah—she'd been drawing the zombies towards her so that the rest of the group could flee, giving them a slightly greater chance of escape.

And they'd taken that chance. They'd taken that chance and they'd ran.

When they looked back, Sarah was already too far gone.

"We could at least do with a car," Clarice said, stretching out her arms.

"We could do with a lot of things," Newbie said. "But we don't exactly have a lot of options right now."

Hayden looked at Clarice as she stood beside him. He half-smiled at her, then tilted his head at Newbie, just like he used to when he was about to have a quiet word with Mum and Dad about something he and Clarice wanted when they were younger.

Clarice half-smiled and nodded, and Hayden jogged after Newbie, his jelly legs barely carrying him.

He walked beside him in silence for a while. In a way, Hayden wanted Newbie to break the quietness. They hadn't discussed Newbie's flip in temper back in the tunnel earlier. Hitting Hayden across the cheek with the axe, a wound that still stung to this moment, but was numbed somewhat by the cold.

But he knew one of them had to address it eventually. And if Newbie wasn't going to be the one to start it, it looked like it was up to Hayden.

"About what happened before. Back in the tunnel. I—"

"It's forgotten. You were only doing what I did when you went after your parents. Trying to stop me."

"It's forgotten," weren't exactly the words Hayden wanted to hear. How about "sorry for smacking you across the face with an axe"?

"I ... Newbie, we're behind you. We've got your back. All of ... both of us. We're here with you. But right now we're exhausted. We've been running all morning. We're lucky we haven't crossed paths with a large group of the zombies, but we won't get lucky so long. And I don't want to be knackered when we do lock horns."

The pair of them walked through the field, Clarice just behind them. Over to the left, flies swarmed around the malnourished remains of a sheep, left out in the cold to starve by its undead farmer.

"When you got that phone call from your parents," Newbie said. "Can you remember how you felt?"

Hayden could remember it all too well. Hope mixed with fear mixed with worry and joy. "Yeah. Just about."

"And can you remember what your thoughts were like at that time? Can you remember how much your mind was filled with that one sole goal: get to my family?"

Hayden couldn't argue with Newbie. "But I heard first hand

from my mum. Not to put a downer on the Warrington transmission, but it's a bit more speculative than an actual—"

"And do you really think your reaction to the call would've been much different if it had been from, say, a neighbour? Some sign of life on your parents' street? Wouldn't you have, like, believed the smallest glimmer of hope if it was right in front of you?"

Hayden wanted to protest, but he knew he couldn't. He couldn't because Newbie had a point. "I guess I would still have tried to find some kind of answer. But—"

"Then there you have it. We need hope, Hayden. I need hope. Otherwise, what's the point in living in this world at all?"

He looked at Hayden when he said that, and Hayden lowered his gaze to the ground. Speaking was helping him keep his mind off his light-headedness and his hunger, so it counted for something.

"I'm sorry about your face. I shouldn't have hit you. But I think you would've done the same if I'd tried to stop you going after your family. And if you had ... well, I think you'd have done the same."

Hayden had an idea what the "and if you had ..." was going to end with. "If you had the balls to stand up to me." And Newbie was right: he was taller and beefier than Hayden, so maybe he'd be unwise to pick a fight with.

But if he'd stopped him trying to save his family? He had no idea what lengths he'd have gone to.

"I feel bad for Sarah," Hayden said. "I ... She held back. For us. I'm not sure if ... I don't know why she'd ..."

He couldn't finish. He didn't want to accept the reality: Sarah had sacrificed herself for the survival of the rest of the group.

"She did a good thing for us," Newbie said. "A horrible but a good thing. And ... and we can't underestimate how different people react in different situations."

"I know she wasn't happy," Clarice cut in.

Her voice made Hayden jump. He hadn't realised she was right behind them. "What do you mean?"

Clarice looked over the fields at the endless hills. "She talked to me a bit. About having nothing to live for. About ... about there being no point to anything anymore. I'm not saying she ... she killed herself. But maybe she, I dunno. Maybe she found her 'point' after all."

Hayden tried to digest his sister's words. He knew Sarah wasn't happy—who *was* happy, after all? But the realisation that she may well have intentionally given up her life ... Hayden wasn't sure how to feel about it.

There was something about Sarah. Something about her that made him feel ... comfortable. And he wasn't ready to let that feeling go just yet.

"Wait, is that a cottage?"

Hayden stopped. He saw his sister squinting into the distance. She pointed her shaky fingers into the middle of nowhere.

Hayden looked too. He couldn't work out where she was looking. "I can't ..."

"Shit," Newbie said. He slowed to a halt. "And is that ... is that a car?"

Hayden searched another few seconds with his myopic eyes and then he saw it.

A grey stone cottage in the middle of the field.

Barbed wire wrapped around the fences.

A Range Rover parked in front of the cottage.

And then, by the door, he saw movement.

Three people emerged from the cottage. Three men. They were wearing thick black body armour and carrying ... were they rifles?

But even more importantly, as the men walked out of the grounds of the house and headed over the field on foot, Hayden noticed they were carrying something else. Something that made him grin.

A can of beans. Each.

"They've got a car," Clarice said. "And ... and they've got food. Are you two thinking what I'm thinking?"

"Unfortunately, yes," Hayden said.

And it was unfortunate. But it was dog eat dog. Every man for themselves. Survival of the fittest.

"I think we're gonna have to pay them a visit," Clarice said.

"A very quiet visit," Hayden said, as the three of them crept slowly down the side of the hill and towards the cottage.

THIRTEEN

Hayden, Newbie and Clarice descended the hill slowly and prayed to whatever god was in the sky that the occupants of the cottage wouldn't get back any time soon.

The hill down to the cottage was slippery and it was impossible to avoid the sound of squelching that their boots made. Hayden kept his eyes on the cottage at all times. He kept his eyes on the leaded windows, looked for a sign of movement, a sign of life inside, but it seemed to be empty.

"So how are we gonna do this?" Newbie asked.

They dropped down the hill and came within metres of the cottage. The trio that had left the cottage were nowhere to be seen anymore. But they could come back at any time. They could come back with their guns. Blast them into oblivion. And that was a risk Hayden wasn't willing to take.

"We've got to go in, take what we can, then get out in the car."

Clarice sighed as they walked past the wooden fences that were lined with barbed wire. "Can't we at least try being diplomatic?"

"They had guns," Hayden said.

"Just like we'd have guns if we were lucky. Come on, bro. There's no need to … to just go in there and steal their livelihood. How would we have liked it if someone had done it to us?"

"They didn't do it to us," Hayden said. "It's … it's just survival."

He walked past Newbie and Clarice and headed towards the front door of the cottage.

There was something weird about this cottage. There were no signs of violence. No evidence that any zombies had even been around here, except for the barbed wire around the tops of the fences. The windows were boarded up with plywood downstairs, but the upstairs windows were empty, vacant. There were no lights on inside. No signs of shadows or movement.

It was like whoever owned the cottage had just taken a long weekend away.

Or at least, Hayden had to hope that was the case.

"Can't we just … just take the car?" Clarice asked.

Hayden stepped up to the cottage door. "With what keys?"

"And what makes you so certain we'll find the keys just lying around in there?"

Hayden put a hand against the door. "I just … I just have a feeling."

Clarice tutted. "Yeah. Right. A feeling. And what makes you so sure the front door will just be…"

She stopped speaking when the front door creaked open as Hayden pushed it aside.

He turned to look at both Clarice and Newbie. Clarice looked shocked. Newbie had narrow eyes. "I don't like this," he said.

"Me neither," Hayden said. He turned and looked into the cottage hallway. "Which is why it's even more important we get this done with."

He held his breath and stepped inside.

His footsteps creaked against the wooden floorboards. There was a faint smell of smoke in the air like a fire had been burning some time ago. There was a warmth to the place, too. A warmth that he hadn't felt in what seemed like forever.

"I could get used to this place," Clarice said.

Her words sparked an idea in Hayden's mind. "Maybe we *could* get used to this place. Four walls. Relatively untouched. Seems pretty safe. What do you—"

"We keep on moving to Warrington," Newbie said, not even giving the idea any thought. "We take some supplies, grab their keys and then we move on to Warrington."

Hayden could feel his idea burst in his face.

They walked over to a door to the left of the stairs and pushed it open. Inside, there was a well-lit kitchen area with clean white tiles and black granite surfaces. There was a delicious smell in the air. A smell like ... like food. All sorts of spices and herbs and ... wow. Hayden could feel his taste buds exploding.

"We take enough to get us through the next two days," Hayden said, as he walked over to a cabinet above the worktop and opened it up. He salivated as tins of beans and tuna stared back at him—and he didn't even like canned tuna. "We ... we don't get over-indulgent."

"I think taking a car qualifies as over-indulgence," Clarice said.

"Well, except for the car."

They grabbed a bunch of tins and cans and shoved as many as they could in their pockets and under their arms. Hayden couldn't help but fantasise over every bit of food he took. Sweetcorn. Tinned mushy peas. Stuff that he would never consider eating warm, let alone cold, in the days before the collapse. But foods that seemed like the most amazing things imaginable right now.

"Any sign of the keys?" Hayden asked.

Newbie searched the drawers around the kitchen. "Plenty of bottle tops. Plenty of old bills and invoices. But no keys."

Hayden scratched at his greasy head. What he'd do for a shower right now. And truth be told, it didn't feel right raiding this place. Clarice was right—this place was somebody else's work, somebody else's haven.

But Newbie hadn't given any of them a choice. They were moving on. There was no sticking around here, as tempting as it was to try and make peace.

Plus, who said these people wanted to make peace at all? Would Hayden want to make peace with a bunch of strangers who'd tried to ransack the bunker but had a change of heart all because they couldn't find the car keys?

"There's other rooms," Hayden said, walking to the door with cans of food stuffed under his arms. "They have to be lying around somewhere."

"Or maybe they aren't lying around at all because they aren't complete idiots and wouldn't leave their car keys on the side in a shitting zombie apocalypse," Clarice said.

Hayden smiled at her. "Right. Sure. Just like they're not stupid enough to leave their front door unlocked in the middle of a zombie apocalypse."

"Did you hear that?"

Newbie's voice caught Hayden's attention. He turned to him, frowned. "Did I hear what?"

Newbie didn't respond. He just looked around the kitchen, slowly.

"Come on," Hayden said, grabbing the kitchen door and trying his best not to drop any of the cans. "We need to find the keys and get the hell out of here. We'll check the lounge first. And then we'll take a look upstairs and—"

"Wait," Clarice said. She walked up to the washing machine and opened up the door.

"Sis, we've hardly got time for laundry, as nice as it would be."

She reached her hand inside the drum. "If you were trying to hide something, you'd choose a place that you *think* would be the least likely place for people to look, right?"

She pulled out a hole-filled old sock that definitely didn't smell like it had been washed any time recently.

"I ... I definitely heard something," Newbie said.

Hayden shook his head. "An unlocked front door and keys stuffed in a spunky old sock. I'm not sure I'd insult their intelligence *that* much ..."

But when Clarice opened up the sock, something tumbled out.

A set of car keys in the palm of her hand.

Hayden stood and stared for a moment. His sister smiled. Newbie kept on looking around the room, uncertain.

"Let's ... let's get out of here," Hayden said. "I don't like this."

"Amen to that."

They rushed out of the kitchen and towards the front door. Hayden could hear creaking now, too. Creaking, like there was somebody else in the cottage after all. Creaking, like they weren't alone.

And then through the front window, well in the distance, he saw the men who had left the cottage returning.

"We ... we need to get out before they—"

Hayden didn't hear the rest of Newbie's words.

An explosion rattled against the wall above the door. Made Hayden's ears ring as he tried to figure out what it was.

He had his answer when he looked over his shoulder and saw a man and a woman, both of them holding pistols, both of them pointing them at Hayden, Newbie and Clarice.

Both of them squeezing their triggers and getting ready to fire another set of bullets.

FOURTEEN

"Please. We... we don't want any trouble. We'll walk right out of here. Forget this ever happened. Please."

Hayden felt his words falling on deaf ears. He stood with his hands in the air as the bald man and the ginger-haired woman at the bottom of the stairs pointed pistols in their direction. Hayden's ears rang from the sound of the gunshot echoing against the wall. The tastes of the foods he'd fantasised about—canned beans, canned peas, canned tuna—had drifted from his mouth, replaced by a familiar tang of fear. An inevitable feeling.

"The car keys," the woman said. She was dressed in a grey Parka coat with a furry hood wrapped around her head. She had grey eyes, which just added to the sense of distrust Hayden felt towards these two people. "Slide them over here."

Hayden looked at Clarice. He didn't want to give up. He didn't want her to comply. But he knew she had to. She had to, to survive. She had to if any of them were to stand a chance of getting out of this one.

She crouched down and pushed the keys to the middle of the

wooden floor. The two gun-wielders just stared at the keys, keeping their guns pointed in Hayden's group's direction.

"We ... we were going to wait," Newbie said. "Wait for you to—"

"Spare us the bullshit," the bald man said, saliva trickling down his unkempt beard. "We heard you talking. Heard your plans."

"Then—then you'll understand. Why we couldn't trust you," Hayden said. "You'll get that. None of us can trust each other anymore. And ... and we weren't going to take all the food—"

"Just the fucking car," the woman said. "Just a few tins, and the fucking car. Hardly anything. Right? Now—now get on your knees and ... and put your hands on the back of your heads."

Hayden saw the woman pull out some thick looking tape and he realised this was the end. There was no bargaining with these people. They were going to tie him and his friends up. They were going to execute them, right here in the hallway of the cottage.

They were going to slaughter them.

Hayden crouched onto his knees but he couldn't give up. He couldn't let himself. "I ... We weren't going to stay here. We heard a transmission. We were going to—to a safe place—"

"Better if you just keep quiet," the man said. He pressed Newbie down and made sure he was on his knees. He didn't make proper eye contact with Hayden or any of the others, like he wasn't comfortable with what he was about to do. "Just—just keep quiet and put your hands behind your backs. All of you."

He wrapped the tape around Newbie's back. Defeat filled Newbie's face. Defeat and acceptance of that defeat.

No. It couldn't end this way. This wasn't how it ended.

The woman stood in front of Hayden. Hayden had to do something. He had to act. He had to get out of here. He wasn't giving up hope. He couldn't give up hope. His life depended on it. His sister's life depended on it.

"Hands behind your back," the woman said.

"We're just like you," Hayden said, as he heard the man wrap tape around his sister's wrists. "We ... we're just like you. Just doing our best to survive. And if we'd known you were here, we wouldn't have bothered you. We wouldn't have—"

"Then you ... you aren't a thing like us," the woman said. And this time, she looked right into Hayden's eyes. "You have no idea what we've done so far to survive. You ... you have no idea of the things we have to do to survive even longer."

Hayden saw a wateriness to the woman's eyes. A glimmer of regret, of fear.

In the distance, he knew the three men would be getting closer. Soon, it would be five on three.

But right now, the odds were in their favour.

"I've had to do bad things too," Hayden said.

The woman blinked and her eyes twitched away again.

Hayden held his breath.

Lunged for the can of tuna he'd dropped to the floor.

Grabbed it and swung it at the gun in the woman's hand.

She dropped it right away and Hayden grabbed it, stood up, wrapped his arms around her neck and held the gun to her temple. The man turned and pointed his gun at Hayden as the woman struggled, trying to wriggle free as Hayden pressed the gun harder and harder.

"Don't ... don't you dare shoot," Hayden shouted. It didn't feel right. It felt like somebody was shouting through him, using him as a vessel. "Don't shoot or I'll ... I'll shoot her. I swear I'll shoot her."

The man kept on pointing his gun at Hayden, his cheeks growing red. Newbie looked on with wide eyes, and Clarice turned from Hayden to Newbie to the man, like it was all some kind of confusing nightmare.

"You ... you wouldn't dare," the woman said.

Hayden pressed his gun harder into the soft cushion of the woman's temple and he heard her wince. "I'll shoot her. If you don't lower your gun and let us—let us leave here with these cans and your car, I'll shoot her."

There was silence between the five of them for some time. Hayden stared into the man's eyes, and the man stared back at him, gun flailing. The woman breathed deeply, tried to struggle free, but Hayden just kept on holding the cold edge of the trigger and pressing the gun closer to the woman's head.

"Let us go," Hayden said. "Untie my friend, my sister, and drop your gun. If you do that, we'll ... we'll let you live. But if you don't. If you don't, I'll ..."

Hayden couldn't even say the words. All of what he was saying felt alien, unreal. And he knew he was doing what he had to do to survive. He knew he was making a horrible call, but a call that had to be made nonetheless. But merely pretending to be a killer was hard enough. Definitely harder than the video games suggested, that was for sure.

The man lowered his gun. "Please. My friends ... they'll be back soon. They'll be back and if they find us like this, they'll—"

"They won't get back here before we're done. So make your choice. Make your choice right this second or I'll ... I'll make it for you."

The man shook his head. He looked at Hayden like he was some kind of monster. Beneath Hayden's grip, the woman kept on wriggling, gasping for air.

"I ... Just let Sammy go."

"Dave, just shoot," the woman said, coughing and gasping. "He's ... don't risk losing the car. Don't risk—"

Hayden covered Sammy's mouth. He didn't want her putting any ideas in Dave's head. "Put your gun on the floor and untie my sister, untie my friend. Then we'll be on our way."

Dave looked at Sammy and shook his head. "I ... I can't—"

"Do it, Dave," Sammy said. "Just ... just do it."

Hayden didn't know what Sammy was encouraging him to do, but he covered her mouth again, covered it despite her teeth biting into his coat, threatening to pierce their way into his fore-arm. "Untie them. Now. Hurry the hell up."

Dave sniffed. He held his shoulders upright. His gun was right by his side now. He stared right into Hayden's eyes. "I'm ... I'm sorry for this. I really am."

And then he lifted the gun and pointed it at Clarice's head.

Hayden didn't even think.

He pulled the gun away from Sammy's head and fired the trigger three, four, five times.

Fired it at Dave's chest, at his neck, into his head.

Dave tumbled to the floor. Blood spurted out of his neck. The top of his skull had blown off but he had a look of shock in his eyes, like the very last thought he'd had was one of amazement, one of awe.

Sammy let out a stunned gasp. She dragged herself away from Hayden's loosening grip and crouched in the pool of blood oozing out of Dave's dead body.

Hayden's hands shook.

He stared at the mess on the floor in front of him.

Stared at the blood, the cracked bone, felt the trigger of the gun underneath his sweaty fingers.

He'd killed a man.

He'd shot a live man dead.

He was a murderer.

FIFTEEN

Ally Harbridge knew something was wrong the second he pushed open the cottage gate and stepped onto the pathway.

"Hold up," he said, raising a hand at Bob. "Something's not right."

He couldn't place exactly what it was that didn't seem right. Not immediately.

And then he saw the rectangular space to his left.

"The car," he said. "Fuckers took the car."

He rushed down the pathway towards the cottage. The front door was ajar. He'd just about had it up to his neck with these pricks back at the cottage. Dave was a decent guy, but Sammy was a handful.

This had to have something to do with Sammy. Probably seduced her way into Dave's fucking pants then tied him up while she plotted her grand escape.

"Wait." Ally felt a hand on his shoulder. He turned around and he saw Bob, sweat pouring down his cheeks, rifle in his other hand. "We should watch out. Could be the flesh-eaters."

Ally pulled his arm away. "Only thing that's fucked up here is that man-eater. But she won't get her teeth into me when I catch her, I swear."

He reached for the door and pushed it open. He heard it creak, echoing against the hallway.

The first thing he noticed was the smell. A metallic stench in the air that had become so familiar since the undead started walking. It was so strong he could taste it, too.

The next thing he noticed was the pool of blood on the floor.

Dave lying in the middle of it.

Ally's stomach sank as he stared at Dave's bloodied body. There was a bullet wound in the side of his head, and his eyes were wide open, like he'd gone through some kind of shock before his death. Rage built up inside Ally. It was that bitch Sammy. He'd been wrong to trust her. All of them had. Fucking naive and ridiculous, right from the start. "Just wait til I—"

"He ... he shot him."

The voice came from the left of the staircase. Took Ally by surprise at first, until he realised it was Sammy.

Tears were rolling down her cheeks. She was holding her shaking, blood-soaked hands to her face.

Ally tensed his jaw. "Tell me what the fuck happened here."

"They ... they took the car," she said. "They came here and—and tried to raid this place. We tried to stop them but ... but things got out of hand. It—it all happened so fast. And ... and then he shot him."

Ally wanted to be annoyed at Sammy. Any excuse to be annoyed at Sammy and he'd take it. But her story added up, in an unfortunate sort of way. There was no car outside the cottage. Which meant somebody else had taken it. "Who was 'he'?"

Sammy sniffed. She stared at the blood pooling out of Dave's corpse, which flies were already beginning to gather around.

Ally bit his lip and marched over to Sammy. He grabbed her by the shoulders and stared her right in her fucking pathetic sad eyes. "Tell me who the fuck—"

"I—I think he was called Hayden," she said. "I think I heard them say Hayden when they were in the kitchen."

"There was more than one of them?"

Sammy drifted off to looking at Dave's body again, her cheeks paling.

Ally smacked her across the face with his knuckles. "Hey. I'm speaking to you. There was more than one?"

"Three," Sammy said, clinching her face. "There ... there were three."

Ally stared at Sammy's begging eyes and he saw his ex-wife, Claudia. Stupid bitch used to always cry like that—like it'd stop Ally being mad with her or something. He didn't mean to be mad or angry at any women—or anyone for that matter. And it annoyed him that he *did* get so pissed off with them.

But hitting them made him feel good. Gave him a kick, just like nicotine gave a smoker, or bungee jumping gave an adrenaline junkie.

"I think they said they're going to a safe place. Somewhere they heard on a transmission."

Ally felt a small weight lift from his shoulders at these words. "They said that? You heard them say that?"

Sammy nodded fast. She sniffed up another bout of snot. "They—they wanted the car so they could get there. I wanted to fight but when I heard they were going there I stopped. I ... I figured there must be another way. I did the right thing. Right?"

Ally wanted to punch Sammy right in her little button nose, send beautiful blood dribbling down over her plump lips and off the edge of her pointy chin. But instead, he put a hand on her shoulder, smiled at her. "I think you've done good," he said. "Thinking outside the box. I like that."

She tried to force a pathetic little smile that Ally just wanted to wipe away, but he held his calm, resisted.

He moved his hand up the side of her soft, sweaty neck. Pinched the end of her silky ginger hair and rubbed it between the tips of his fingers. "And when you're good, you know what that means, don't you?"

Her eyes lit up and Ally just loved it. Loved the spark of life. The spark of hope that he dangled in front of her like a toffee-coated carrot on an orgasm-inducing stick. "Can ... can I see him?"

Ally moved his hand further up the side of her head. He heard Bob tutting and struggling at the door. He didn't approve too much of Ally's methods, but he put up with them. Mutual respect, that sort of thing. "Depends on whether our new friends get to Warrington or not," he said. He moved close to Sammy's ear, felt the heat coming off her skin. "If they do, then you can see your boy again."

He grabbed her breast, squeezed it so tight that it made Sammy wince.

"If they don't, then you've got a lot of explaining to do. As for your kid, well ... we'll find a way to have our fun with him."

Ally felt the heat from Sammy's cheeks dip in a split second.

Heard a little whimper from the back of her throat.

He smiled.

* * *

SARAH TRIED NOT to cry out from under the sweaty, shit-tasting gag as the big man called Bob held her by the door and the other man called Ally put his hands all over the terrified woman in the cottage.

All she could think about was Hayden, Newbie, Clarice.

The Warrington transmission.

Home to these people.

The place they were heading.

SIXTEEN

Hayden leaned against the back seat and tried all he could to stop shaking.

Newbie was driving the Range Rover they'd taken from the cottage. His sister was beside Hayden in the back. But it didn't feel like they were there, not really. It felt like he was alone. Alone with the knowledge of what he'd done.

He'd shot a man.

Murdered him.

But there was another bit of knowledge creeping back into his awareness, rearing its ugly head. A bit of knowledge he didn't want to accept, or even think about.

But it was coming dangerously close to sneaking over the surface.

"You did what you had to do," Clarice said, as she stared out of the condensation-covered window of the Range Rover. "I ... I'd have died if you hadn't shot that man. You saved my life."

She turned to Hayden. Half-smiled. But although he felt the sincerity in her words, he could sense his little sister looking at him differently. Looking at him like he was a killer.

If only she knew.

"What we did," Hayden said. "Taking the stuff from the cottage. Taking this car. It ... it was wrong. You were right about that."

Clarice shrugged. "They turned out dicks anyway. So that makes it a little more okay."

"It doesn't make anything okay. I killed a man. It ... it shouldn't have to be that way. We shouldn't have to kill each other to survive."

"Always been that way, brother," Newbie said, glancing in the rearview mirror at Hayden as rain lashed down on the windscreen. "Always been that way."

Hayden wanted to have another swipe at Newbie but he knew doing so was unfounded. He understood the root of his frustrations, now. The source of his behaviour.

"If you hadn't shot him, we'd probably all have died—"

"I killed Mum," Hayden said.

Clarice went quiet. She narrowed her eyes, searched Hayden's face. "I know you put her to rest. You told me you—"

"She was alive," Hayden said, the words spilling out of his mouth like water from a leaky pipe. "I ... I went to put her down and she was alive. She spoke to me."

"No," Clarice said.

"She ... she told me to put her down. And ... and not to tell you because—"

"Don't lie about things like this, Hayden."

"I'm not lying," Hayden said, raising his voice. His hands shook even more, and nausea filled his empty stomach. "I ... I held her hand and then I held a pillow over her face. I waited til she went quiet, til she stopped struggling, and then I took the pillow away and I—"

"You wouldn't," Clarice said, shaking her head. Her eyes were watery and filled with tears. "You ... you wouldn't do that to Mum. You couldn't. None of us could."

"I did, Sis," Hayden said, his voice quivery. "I did it. And ...

and I guess I've wanted to say something all along but I just … I just wanted to protect you. I didn't want you to know the truth because the truth hurts. But I did it because she asked me to. I did it because there was no other way."

Tears streamed down Clarice's cheeks. Newbie kept on glancing in the rearview mirror, but he was keeping himself to himself as he focused on the rain-battered road.

"She … you say she spoke. You—you didn't give me a chance. To say goodbye. You didn't give me a chance to—"

"Because you're my little sister and it's my duty to look out for you," Hayden said. "And you wouldn't have liked what I did. What I had to do. You wouldn't have liked seeing Dad in the state he was in. You … you would've had to deal with the sound of their fucking necks cracking, the feel of the life drifting out of both of them …" His voice gave way completely for a few seconds, and he had to regain his breath. "I couldn't let you live with witnessing that. I just couldn't."

Clarice looked like she was about to say something else through her tear-soaked lips, but she just closed her mouth and turned away to look out of the smeared window.

Hayden stared at her. Looked at her greasy dark hair, her skinny frame. Always a skinny kid. Probably something to do with her hatred for any of the foods Mum and Dad used to serve for them. At one stage, measures got so desperate that she was literally eating a bowl of Coco Pops without milk three meals a day. It was Hayden who finally convinced her to eat more and more, step by step. Told her eating her greens would make her even prettier.

She took to it, held on to Hayden's word, like she always did. And remarkably enough, eating those greens did keep on making his lovely little sister prettier.

She'd had every reason to trust him.

Except now.

Hayden didn't say anything else to Clarice. He didn't want to push her buttons too hard. She needed time. Time to understand.

Time to get her head around what he'd told her. And he wasn't proud of what he'd told her. He wanted to keep it from her. Keep her wrapped in cotton wool for as long as the pair of them survived.

But he felt better. Just getting the confession off his chest made him feel free.

He just hoped to God that feeling free was a good enough return for the short-term shattering of his sister's emotions.

Hayden leaned forward and looked through the front windscreen. "How we doing?"

Newbie side-glanced at him. He cleared his throat. "Doing just fine. Should be at Warrington in forty minutes or so at this rate. Providing we don't run into any obstructions. Or worse —infected."

Hayden nodded. He stared at the tall evergreen trees either side of them. There was no sign of any zombie apocalypse going on at all out here in the countryside, but for the occasional piece of loose rubble on the road, or a fallen tree that Newbie had to swerve the car around, unsorted in this new world lacking any kind of emergency services. "We've done alright to now. You ... your kid. D'you know whereabouts in Warrington they lived?"

"Eighteen Astley Road. Just on the outskirts. Google Street Viewed it enough times. Hell, I even turned up a few times. Thought about walking in there, wrapping my arms around my Amy. Couldn't bring myself to do it. Couldn't strike up the nerve. Probably for the best considering the restraining order. But not anymore."

Hayden patted Newbie lightly on his shoulder and leaned back into the car. He didn't want to argue with Newbie about the risks of going somewhere just outside the centre of a town. But it wasn't just because of the risk of military and undead. It was because sometimes, it was better to keep the past in the past. A part of Hayden wished he'd never gone back home—as cruel as that was to his dying mum, his zombie dad, and his terrified sister.

But it was just a small part of him. A small part that niggled away like a stubborn spot, resistant to the squeeze.

"You ... you did the right thing," Clarice said.

Hayden turned around. He wasn't sure he'd heard correctly.

Clarice was staring ahead at the front of the car, but it didn't really look like she was focusing on anything in particular.

"I ... What do you—"

"With Dad and ... and Mum. You did a brave thing. And you came for me. Got me out of that house. I ... Thank you."

She turned to Hayden. This time, she smiled at him with warmth, smiled at him like she always used to smile at him when they were both kids. When he'd bought her a lolly from the school tuck shop, when he'd helped her with her maths homework.

He smiled back at her and then he heard the thud.

"Shit," Newbie said.

Hayden spun around. Newbie was struggling with the steering wheel, lifting his foot up and down on the accelerator. "What is it?"

But Newbie didn't have to answer.

The engine thudded again, again, again.

The Range Rover slowed to a halt, right in the middle of the torrential rain.

And in the silence, beyond the sound of the rain pattering against the metal car roof, Hayden heard the echoing gasps of the undead ...

SEVENTEEN

"Can you fix it?" Clarice asked.

Newbie leaned into the bonnet of the Range Rover. Rain lashed down from the grey storm clouds above. The smell of damp soil was strong in the air—a smell that took Hayden back to his childhood holidays in the New Forest. Always rained, always. But he kind of liked it. Liked that smell. It was fresh.

Which made a pleasant change to the usual rotting stench of the undead.

Newbie sighed. He wiped the rain from his face. "It's the apocalypse. What d'you reckon my chances of fixing it are?"

Hayden stared into the evergreen trees at the opposite side of the long road. They cordoned them in on either side. There was no escaping them. Just a long road between them and trees that stretched into the sky like watchful gods, watchful demons.

And beyond the first of the trees, Hayden could hear the echoing groans of an oncoming army of dead.

"We're gonna have to move on foot," Newbie said.

"There's still a chance we can get back," Hayden said. "Head back the way we came. Go towards the cottage and—"

"Not a chance," Newbie said, shaking his head. "We're closer to Warrington than we are the cottage. Journey ain't so far from here. We can push on. But we'd better get a move on."

He turned his back on Hayden and Clarice and started walking down the middle of the road, leaving the Range Rover abandoned and stacked with the tins of food they'd risked so much to get their hands on.

Hayden looked at Clarice, waited for some kind of answer, some kind of decision.

She stared at the trees behind Hayden. She could hear them too, he knew that. The mass of dead. The dead that would be upon them at any given moment—not when they least expected it, because they had to be constantly prepared in a world like this. But they'd be here soon. They'd be here, and Hayden, Clarice and Newbie would be running again.

Always running.

"I think ... we can't separate," Clarice said. "Not after how far we've come."

Hayden looked at Newbie as he charged down the central lines of the road. The rain dripped from his torn black coat. Hayden could feel the rain on his lips and he licked it, the freshest water he'd tasted in days. "He's blinded by this idea of his kid being in Warrington. I ... I just don't see how we can go marching into another town."

"And weren't you blinded when you thought I was alive? When you heard Mum's voice on the phone, weren't you following the road purely on faith?"

"Yeah, but—"

"He walked into my house just after you, brother. As good as by your side. And he's still here right now. We ... we lost Sarah. We left her behind when we could've done more for her. We can't leave Newbie to find his own path too."

Hayden wanted to tell his sister that he just wanted to keep her safe. That he personally would follow Newbie, but with his sister it was just too much of a risk. He couldn't put her life in danger. He couldn't be there when another family member died.

Or, he couldn't die on his one remaining close relative.

He couldn't do that.

He was about to say something when he saw the branches of the evergreen trees rustle just over Clarice's shoulder.

He looked at the spot where he'd seen the movement. A definite shaking of the leaves. And there was still that low, echoing hum of the gasps, the groans.

Clarice turned around slowly. "What is—"

"Ssh," Hayden said. "We ... we need to get away from here. We need to ..."

And then the smell hit him.

Damp.

Rotting.

Death.

He grabbed his sister's hand and went to grip on the mallet ... only he realised it wasn't there. There was the gun. The gun he'd shot the guy called Dave at the cottage with. It was in his pocket, but firing at the zombies would be too loud.

He had to get back to the car and get a weapon.

He had to ...

He saw the first of the zombies stagger out from behind the trees. It was short, skinny. Male. Bones stuck out of the pale flesh on its bitten ribcage. Its eyes looked like they were in two different shades, but then Hayden realised that's because one of them had a bite mark on it that had sent eye fluid trickling down the poor thing's face.

He stepped to the right when he saw more rustling in the trees.

To the right.

Further to the right.

And to the left.

Clarice tightened her grip on Hayden's hand. "We need to go."

And Hayden knew she was right. Zombies flooded out of the trees opposite them. Lots of them—ten, twenty, more. All of them staggering in his direction, in his sister's direction, in ...

He looked up the road.

Newbie was still marching down it.

Marching down, facing forward, the trees rustling beside him too.

Hayden wanted to shout and then he heard the rustling to the right.

Heard the gasps, the footsteps getting faster, smelled another bout of rotting flesh.

He turned to his right and he saw the zombies coming out of the trees on the right now, too.

A mass of zombies coming from the left, the right, from all around.

"What ... what do we do?" Clarice asked. And she said it in a fearful way that terrified Hayden. Gripped his hand like she used to when they were kids and begged him for an answer.

And he always had an answer. He always had some words or some solution to pick Clarice up, to give her strength, give her confidence.

But as the zombies piled out of the trees on both sides of the road, Hayden didn't have an answer.

And that's what terrified him more than anything.

EIGHTEEN

Hayden sprinted down the open road away from the emerging mass of zombies.

He held his sister's hand tightly. Felt cold sweat trickling from her palm onto his. Up ahead, he saw Newbie turn around and look at the zombies as they staggered out of the trees, staggered from both directions, getting closer and closer.

He could hear their footsteps. Hear their gasps and their growls. It was a noise that he'd never get used to. A sound that would always ring in his ears, set his mind on fire. And right now, there was nothing any of them could do but run. The car was surrounded and broken down. All the food they'd gathered from the cottage and the handheld weapons they'd acquired—except for the axe Newbie was holding and the gun in Hayden's pocket —were gone.

Right now, all they had were their feet.

All they could do was run.

Hayden felt his sister slowing down as she ran beside him. He felt pains aching, creeping through his body as the mass of rotting undead pursued them, just like they'd keep on pursuing them until the very end. He wondered how many people had died this way. Died running, filled with fear and adrenaline, tripping over a lace or cocking over and made themselves zombie food.

Gasps and growling and footsteps getting closer, closer ...

"We need to go into the woods," Hayden shouted, abandoning his silence policy now it was glaringly obvious the zombies knew exactly where he was anyway.

Newbie kept on running. He shook his head but didn't look back. "Not ... not far down this road. Need to keep going. Nearly there."

Hayden glanced over his shoulder and regretted it instantly. The pack of zombies was so dense that it was filling up the road. He could just about make out the abandoned Range Rover through their mass, but it was barely noticeable.

So many of them.

Flesh spewing out of their red-raw limbs.

Maggots biting into their decaying skulls.

All chasing, all approaching.

"Shit," Hayden said, as he kept on running, kept on holding his sister's hand. "We ... Sis, we need to go into the woods. Need to try and lose them."

"But they *came* from the woods," Clarice said.

Hayden looked at the trees on his left. He could see movement, rustling. A sign that more zombies were preparing to join their companions. Readying themselves to hunt.

Then he looked to the right and he saw the branches and the leaves were still.

"I think we can go right," Hayden said, cold sweat dripping down his face. "We can go into the woods and lose them if—"

"But what about Newbie?"

Hayden looked ahead at Newbie. Looked at him striding away. And a part of Hayden saw himself in Newbie. He saw himself making his stupid, life-threatening decisions when he'd gone back to the bombarded Preston to try and save his family.

He saw himself, and yet he saw exactly what those decisions had done for him.

Those decisions had saved his sister.

"He's made his choice. There's nothing we can say to change his mind now."

Hayden gripped Clarice's hand tighter.

"But ... we can't just ..."

"I'm sorry, Sis," Hayden said. And he was. He really was. Newbie was a good man. He was a man who'd been there for him all this time, except for their occasional spats that could be forgiven in the circumstances.

But he was a man with a mission of his own. A man with a journey, a quest, to pursue.

A quest that he had to see out alone, because following him was just too much danger for Hayden to risk putting himself in right now.

Way too much risk putting Clarice in.

"Not too late to take a right," Hayden shouted. "You ... you know where we'll be. You know where we'll be if you need us."

Newbie didn't turn around. He didn't nod. He just kept on moving, kept on speeding up the road.

Hayden's stomach sank, but he couldn't let himself be sentimental anymore.

He tightened his grip on his sister's hand and pulled her to the trees at the right of the road.

As he moved towards the evergreen leaves, he prepared to be swarmed in the clutches of zombies he hadn't seen hiding away, waiting to pursue their prey.

He held his breath as he sprinted at the trees.

Took one final look at Newbie.

Then the leaves and the branches scratched against Hayden's face and the woods surrounded him.

The pair of them ran through the trees in no real direction and with no real end point in mind. Just getting away from the zombies was a good enough goal in itself. Hayden's shoes snapped against loose twigs, splashed through thick mud, and he lost his balance a few times and almost dragged Clarice down with him.

But they were alive. They were alive, and the sounds of the zombies' gasps were getting gradually less pronounced behind them.

Hayden slowed down his running when he was pretty certain the rotting stench was far enough out of his senses. He let go of his sister's hand and rested his palms on his knees. His heart pounded, and a crippling stitch gnawed at his stomach and chest.

He could hear his sister panting, puffing beside him. And although she sounded like she was exhausted, like everything was a struggle, it was just a relief to hear her breathing.

Hayden never let go of how lucky he was. Never.

"So I guess we'll have to find a diverted route to Warrington?" Clarice said.

Hayden looked up at the sky. He was pretty certain they hadn't veered too far off the track, but he couldn't know for definite. "I ... I think if we head west from here we'll be parallel with the road again," he said. "We just ... we just have to stay quiet. Move slower. Keep our guard up."

"So Warrington's definitely still the destination?"

Hayden thought about it. He tried to picture another possible destination now that the bunker had been overrun, and he realised just how out of options they were. Wanderers. Nothing but wanderers, with a distant hope of a safe place in Warrington in the back of their mind.

"I guess we don't have a choice," he said. He walked past Clarice and led the way through the thick trees.

"Whatever happened to ladies first?" she asked.

"Looking out for my sister happened to ladies first."

And then he stopped.

He stopped because he heard twigs to his left.

Twigs snapping.

Footsteps.

"I don't remember you being so witty—"

"Ssh," Hayden said. He held out a hand. Searched the thick leaves of the trees beside him, but couldn't see any signs of movement. "You ... you hear that?"

Clarice frowned. "Hear what?"

Hayden thought maybe he'd been imagining things. Maybe it was just his mind screwing with him.

And then he heard the twigs snapping again.

And this time, he heard the gasps somewhere beyond the twigs.

He became suddenly aware of just how vulnerable he was. Without a weapon—or at least, a weapon that didn't frigging blast like a gun. Without a weapon and all alone in the woods.

He took his sister's hand. "We need to get out of here. We need to—"

And then he saw the leaves rustle in front of him.

Saw the branches shake.

He tensed his fists.

Prepared to take on whatever was coming his way.

Newbie tumbled out from the branches, panting, sweating, shaking.

Hayden stared at him in disbelief. His stomach was still going, and his tensed fists had turned to jelly. "Newbie, what—"

"You two might wanna try keeping your voices down," Newbie said. He looked up and pointed a thumb over his shoulder. "I think I've driven our friends off the road. But the bad thing is they're heading our way."

Hayden listened to the sounds of the oncoming footsteps, smelled the scent of death, and he readied himself for another bout of running.

* * *

ALLY WALKED down the centre of the country lane and he knew the dead couldn't be too far ahead.

The stench of them was still strong in the cold winter air. Smelled like shit. No: way, way worse than shit. Rotting shit mixed with rotting piss smelled with all kinds of awful.

But he knew the living had been here, too.

He walked along the road, Bob, Sammy and the gagged bitch whose name they still hadn't figured out beside them. The sun poked from behind the thick grey clouds, which were like smoke from an addict's lungs. The zombies were like a cancer that hung over their every living moment.

He could go places with similes and metaphors, especially when there was jack all else to do these days.

They stopped beside the Range Rover. Ally recognised it right away. The bonnet had got a bit dusty and muddied, and there were things inside—tins, cans, stuff like that—which weren't there beforehand. He could smell burning from the engine. Always did mess up like that. A problem he'd had ever since he first bought the thing.

Luckily for him, he knew how to fix it.

He turned to Bob, Sammy and the gagged woman and he pointed at the car. "Throw her in the boot. I'll get this up and running."

The brunette's eyes widened as Bob and Sammy opened up the boot of the Range Rover and tossed her inside. He heard the crack of her face against the hard laminate flooring he'd put in there. He kind of liked it.

Used to throw Claudia in there when she pissed him off. Locked her in there for the night. He'd had it custom fitted so a little section acted as a cage. Trapped whoever was in there in complete darkness.

He used to go to sleep to the sounds of her crying and screaming.

Didn't matter. Lived way out in the countryside. Bitch could scream all she wanted.

Bob and Sammy closed the boot and walked over to Ally, who leaned on the bonnet.

"What d'you think it means?" Sammy asked, reluctance in her voice.

Ally looked up at her as he reached into the engine. Smiled. "It means they're on course for Warrington. And it means we're gonna be there to welcome them."

NINETEEN

They ran further and further through the woods, and it didn't take them long to get lost.

Hayden stopped and rested his hands on his aching knees. The sound of the cold wind whistled through the trees as Clarice and Newbie panted beside him. Hayden had never been the fittest of people. Probably the healthiest period of his life was back in high school when he was actually forced into doing physical activity. But even then, he found ways to worm out of the classes. Stubbed toes, dodgy knees, things like that.

He regretted the day he'd ever lied about having dodgy knees now he knew what actual knee ache felt like.

"Sounds like we've lost 'em," Newbie said. It threw Hayden to see him standing still for once. He'd kind of got used to Newbie powering onwards, no matter what. He could sympathise with Newbie's plight to find his daughter. Sympathise, but lament it at the same time.

"I'm not so sure being lost is such a good idea," Clarice said. She looked around, examined the trees as they shook in the whirring wind. Hayden tried to listen for gasps, groans and footsteps, but there was nothing.

And sometimes, nothing was the eeriest sound of all.

Newbie took a few deep breaths and carried on walking. "We can't be too far off route."

"I admire your confidence," Clarice said, as she started to hobble on after Newbie.

"I never insisted you joined me," Newbie said. "I never forced you here."

"Let's not go there again," Hayden said. He struggled to catch his breath and tried not to tumble over with how dizzy he was feeling. "We just ... we just need to focus on getting to Warrington now. And getting there in one piece."

"We're already torn into pieces," Clarice said. "Sarah isn't here."

Clarice had a point. Hayden had been trying not to think too much about Sarah. About what she'd given up to try and help the rest of the group. It was a sacrifice he wasn't sure he'd be able to make given the opportunity.

A sacrifice he'd make for nobody but his family.

They waded through the trees and over the fallen leaves, which crunched beneath their feet. "Newbie's right," Hayden said, trying to change the subject. "We ... we can't be too far from Warrington. Even if we went way off route, I'm pretty sure we were still heading in the same direction as we were on the road."

"Again, your blind faith impresses me," Clarice said, as she stepped over a pile of broken twigs. "I wish I could share it."

They walked further. It felt like hours, but in truth it could only have been minutes. They tried to stay headed in the same direction, but it was hard to keep track when there were nothing but trees around them, sky above them. Hayden tried to use the sun as some kind of marker—he knew it rose in the east and set in the west—but he couldn't even keep track of that right now, as it peeked through the grey clouds directly above them.

He had to face the truth. Accept the truth, as a cold shiver wrapped around him.

He was lost. They were all lost.

What felt like another hour later, Clarice asked if they could take a breather. But Newbie insisted they had to keep pushing on. They couldn't hang around. It was afternoon, it was winter and it was Britain, which meant that the sun would be setting in a matter of hours.

They didn't want to get caught out here when night fell. That was good for nobody. Nobody but the cold.

And the zombies.

They were walking for a while longer, Hayden's legs feeling like they were going to shatter to pieces with every step, when Newbie stopped.

He lifted up a hand and halted Hayden and Clarice's progression. Hayden swore he could hear Newbie's pulsating heart cutting through his raspy breaths. Hayden stayed still. Waited for Newbie to reveal what it was he'd stopped them for. He looked at the trees as they rustled in the wind. He saw patterns. Patterns, shapes, all moving. He thought he heard gasps, thought he heard footsteps.

Keep your cool. Just keep your cool. All okay. Nothing in here.

"What ... what is it?" Clarice asked.

"Up ahead," Newbie said. "Look. Do you see it?"

Hayden squinted and once again wished he'd paid a visit to an optician before the world went to shit. "I don't—"

"That ... that house. The red brick. A detached house. Like ... like my ex-wife's house. Like Amy's house."

Hayden could hear the crackling in Newbie's voice. He turned slowly to his sister and she raised her eyebrows, and Hayden raised his eyebrows in turn. He looked back at where Newbie was looking and this time, he saw it—saw the new-looking wooden fence surrounding a back garden, saw the red brick of the modern house that had obviously been designed to look like it was from another era. In the upstairs window, he saw an England football flag, except there wasn't just the red of the England flag cutting through it—there was the red of blood splashed over the white material.

"It's ... is this Warrington?" Clarice asked.

Newbie stepped forward. "My Amy. There was a house like this on her road. Lots of houses like this. And ... and there was a woods. There was a woods. I have to go find her. I have to go—"

"Wait," Hayden said. He caught up with Newbie. He couldn't believe their luck. And that's part of what made him feel doubtful about all this; what gave him a niggling sense of unease of *something* not quite being right. "We need to go slowly out of the woods. We need to ..."

But then Newbie did something completely unexpected to Hayden.

He pushed away his hands and he ran.

Hayden didn't know what to do at first. He just stood there, frozen, watching as Newbie sprinted out of the woods towards the road where his family supposedly lived.

"Do we chase him?" Clarice asked.

Hayden sighed. He heard the shaking of the leaves, the pattering noises that were like footsteps. "I don't think we have a choice."

He took his sister's hand and the pair of them ran after Newbie and towards the road.

The further they ran, the more Hayden noticed the trees around them thinning out. And as they thinned out, he could see more houses—houses and cars and gardens and a little winding cul-de-sac, all untouched, all quiet, but all undoubtedly dead.

He wanted to shout out for Newbie as he watched him run down the middle of the street and towards another clump of these modern houses. He wanted to, but he didn't want to risk waking this sleepy road. Because the dead would come. The dead were somewhere, and eventually, they always came.

So he just had to run. Just had to follow Newbie. Just had to hope.

Eventually, Newbie took a right and ran across the well-trimmed grass of a small detached house. He threw himself into the white front door and shook at the handle, then when he realised it was locked he stepped back and swung the axe at the window once, twice, three times, every blow louder than the last.

Hayden thought he saw movement in the corners of his eyes at the end of the street.

He thought he smelled death.

Newbie disappeared through the smashed window and Hayden heard his footsteps banging against the floor inside, heard him racing up the stairs. And he prayed for him. Prayed he wouldn't find anything similar to what Hayden had found—one of his parents bitten and dying, another one already dead.

"I—I think I just saw something," Clarice said.

She was looking to her left at a wire fence that had been ripped into two. There was a thick green hedge behind it, and beyond it Hayden got the sense that somebody was there, somebody was watching.

"They ... they made it out."

Newbie's voice took Hayden by surprise. He swung around, realised Newbie was standing at an opened upstairs window. He had a note in his shaking hand. A note that was covered in blood. He was staring at it with wide eyes. "To ... to the safe haven," he said. "They left. They made it."

Hayden definitely heard footsteps to his right. He heard the echoing of a groan, too. He didn't see anything on the road, but he could see the faintest outline of movement in the lounge windows of the detached houses.

The awoken dead.

"That's ... that's great," he said, turning back to Newbie. "But you need to get out of there now. You ... We need to push on."

Newbie looked at Hayden. He half-smiled. Tears filled his eyes. "Yeah," he said, gripping the note loosely in his hand. "Yeah. We do."

He turned around and a zombie flew at him.

Newbie shouted out. Pushed at the zombie, tried to get it away.

But it wasn't going away.

It stuck its teeth into Newbie's shoulder.

Newbie tumbled back, fell out of the window, a shower of blood from his own bitten flesh sprinkling down with him.

He hit the concrete of the drive outside his house with an echoing crack.

He let out a pained moan.

Down the road, a window smashed open.

TWENTY

Hayden could only stand and stare in shock as blood spurted out of Newbie's mouth and trickled out of the bite wound on his shoulder.

But he couldn't stand and stare for long because a group of zombies were heading down the road in his direction.

"Newbie!" Clarice shouted. Hayden could sense that all her inhibitions had dropped, and all she cared about right now was making sure that Newbie was okay. Well, not okay, but comfortable at the very least.

She threw herself in Newbie's direction.

Hayden grabbed her arm.

"We ... We have to go," he said. Down the road, the zombies got closer, snapping away at the air, their pace getting faster. "We have to get out of here."

She struggled with Hayden's grip, smacked his hand away. Tears trickled down her cheeks. "Don't ... just don't do your brotherly thing on me now. He's ... It's Newbie, Hay. It's Newbie."

Hayden looked over at Newbie as he gasped and gargled blood. His face had turned a nasty shade of purple. He hadn't noticed it at first, but one of Newbie's arms had snapped completely and contorted to the right.

Contorted to the right with that little note he'd found in his daughter's house—the note that filled him with such optimism and relief as he'd looked through the window and smiled—still in between his fingers.

The axe was in his other hand, but he'd been too late to use it.

But it could come in handy for Hayden.

Hayden looked back at the oncoming zombies. There were ten of them, and all of them were moving fast. All blood-soaked, all rotting, all powering down the middle of the road. Behind them, in the windows of other detached houses, Hayden could see more undead moving and scrapping about. Soon, they'd join the ten in the road and that ten would become twenty, that twenty would become thirty.

Which meant they had to act. Quick.

Hayden ran across the garden of Newbie's ex-wife's house and joined his sister by Newbie's side. She was holding his hand and crying, muttering reassuring words to him. But the wound on his shoulder was bad. It was a bite wound for one, so that was bad enough in itself. A bite wound meant one thing and one thing only, and there was no escaping the outcome.

Newbie was bitten. Which meant he was going to turn.

Hayden crouched down beside Newbie and put a hand on his chest. The echoing cries of the zombies on the road behind them got nearer, and Hayden even thought he could hear more rustling from the opposite side of the road.

He looked into Newbie's wide eyes and he felt himself tearing up. He'd pictured saying goodbye to his friend a few times, in those dreams that haunted his sleep, but it was always more Hollywood style. He had all the time in the world to say goodbye, to put down the ones he loved peacefully, in his visions. A swift blow to the head and then nothing.

But killing his mum had taught him that there was nothing romantic or dignified about death.

"I'm sorry," Hayden said, as he reached over for the axe in Newbie's weakened fingers. "I'm sorry but you ... you know what I have to do. You know what I have to do."

Newbie stared up at him, speechless, with tears in his blood-shot eyes. There was fear there too. Fear, but a weird kind of acceptance, as he coughed up more blood, winced with pain.

The zombies were just metres away now.

Hayden took the axe from Newbie's hand and he lifted it over Newbie's head. Clarice cried. She didn't protest, she didn't try to put up a fight, she just cried. Cried and apologised to Newbie, apologised for him being bitten, for them being separated, for him not finding his daughter, for everything.

Hayden held his breath as the horrid tingling sensation engulfed his stomach.

Just get it done with. Get it over with. Nice and quick.

And then he brought the axe swinging down onto Newbie's neck as hard as he could.

He felt Newbie's blood splash up over his face. Hayden grunted in horror, his heart raced and the fear of the lazy layabout he used to be reared its head all over again.

He heard Newbie splutter, heard a little whooshing sound as blood filled his windpipe, and then he swung the blade at Newbie's neck again.

This time, he didn't have any chance to feel any more fear, or even stick around to see whether he'd properly finished Newbie off.

It was only when he'd delivered the final blow that he remembered he had a gun in his pocket.

He stood up and turned around just as the first of the zombies flew itself at him.

He steadied his footing and swung the blood-splattered axe right into the side of its face.

And then another one, a shorter one, rushed for Hayden's leg and Hayden swung down on the back of its head and knocked it to the road.

He knew blows to the face and the head weren't enough to deal with these zombies, but they held them off. And that's all he had the time to do now—hold them off, keep them away.

A small gap formed between the first two zombies bleeding out on the road and the rest of the growing pack. More windows smashed and cracked, and more groans joined the choir.

"Quick," Hayden said, taking his sister's hand even though he knew she hated it. "Through the fence."

"It's blocked, it's—"

Hayden knew what his sister was talking about when he looked at the opening in the wire fencing at the bottom of the road. There were three zombies all forcing their way through it. One of them, a ginger man with freckles all over his face, hadn't quite grasped the way the fence worked, and was pushing himself so hard into the wire that it was slicing through his exposed stomach.

"We need to—to get inside," Clarice said. "Get inside a house before—before it's too late."

Hayden swung around as another zombie pummelled towards him. He cracked it across the jaw with the axe, felt more blood cover his body, and turned to the house where Newbie's daughter lived. "We need to get into a garden and over one of those fences," he said.

And then with his sister's hand in his, he ran.

Clarice veered in the direction of the house. "But there might be more at the other side of the—"

"They'll find a way into the house. We're just cornering ourselves if we go in there. They'll find a way in. They always do."

"But I ... I'm scared, Hay. I'm scared."

"So am I, Sis," Hayden said, as the pair of them ran towards the gate at the side of Newbie's ex's house, the wooden fence at the back of the garden just low enough for them to climb over. "So am I."

Hayden wanted to turn back and look at Newbie one final time. But he couldn't. Not just because tons of zombies were nipping at their heels, but because he couldn't see Newbie sprawled out on the driveway, his head dangling on by a few pieces of tendon. He couldn't see Newbie that way, because that wasn't the Newbie he'd been friends with. That wasn't the Newbie who had stood by his side and fought together with him.

He looked down at the crumpled piece of paper he'd taken from Newbie's hand. Saw the note written on it in what must've been Newbie's ex-wife's handwriting: *Riversford Industrial Estate. Safe place there. If anyone's reading this, that's where we've gone. x*

And then he held his breath, held his sister's hand extra tightly, and threw himself at the top of the fence.

He was at the top and ready to climb over when he heard the wood split.

TWENTY-ONE

Hayden felt the fence snap beneath his feet the second he and his sister reached the top of it.

As he fell to the ground below, he imagined breaking his leg or contorting his arm just like Newbie had. He imagined not being able to do anything as he lay on the floor, as the teeth of the dead sunk into his flesh.

But worse, he imagined his sister being stuck without a weapon, surrounded by zombies, and Hayden having no way of helping her, of saving her.

Hayden hit the road with a thump. He felt his face stinging, but he was okay on the whole. He quickly spun around to check his sister was okay—she was already on her feet and starting to run again. Beyond the split fence behind them, Hayden could hear the heavy footsteps of the rotting corpses coming in their direction.

There was no time to stick around, not anymore.

Hayden stood up and dug into his pocket as he ran across the open section of the road and past more detached houses. It was quiet, free of zombies, and that was a positive in itself. It didn't matter that there was a group of them onto their scent, there wasn't any more blocking the road. Small positives in the grand scheme of things.

He pulled the gun out of his pocket and handed it to Clarice. "You need to use this. If anything happens. If … if you're surrounded, you need to use this."

Clarice frowned and stared at it as they ran further along the road. "I—I don't think I—"

"Just take it. Don't fire it willy-nilly. But fire it when you absolutely need to. Whenever that is."

Clarice took the gun, and Hayden had a horrible image of his sister holding the gun to her head after being gnawed by a zombie on one of her legs. Pulling the trigger.

No. He couldn't let that happen. He wasn't going to let that happen.

"Are they close?" Clarice asked.

Hayden didn't even want to look. He knew they were chasing them, but he didn't want to see them. Seeing them was accepting defeat. Seeing them was accepting that the undead were after them, and the very fact that they were after them meant that they were going to catch up with them.

It was just a matter of time.

The living tired far more easily than the dead.

They reached the exit of the cul-de-sac and Hayden looked down at the crumpled note in his hand. "Riversford Industrial Estate," he said. "That's where the safe place is."

"Great load of help in the middle of a town that we've never pissing visited."

"But we have a name. We have a location. A destination. That's … that's something."

He wanted to tell Clarice that they had the story about Newbie to tell his daughter, too. How hard her dad had fought to get to her. How he'd … how he'd fought right until the very end, given it all he had.

But how he'd failed to make it.

Failed, like so many others.

"Take a right and head into those trees," Hayden said, pointing across the road.

"I'm just about sick of trees."

"I don't see what other option we—"

"Hey! Help! Give us a hand here! Please!"

The voice came from the cul-de-sac Hayden and Clarice had just come from.

Clarice started to turn around and looked back but Hayden stopped her. "Don't. Don't pay any attention. We need to move on."

Clarice frowned at Hayden. "There's—there's people back there. People who need help—"

"*We* need help," Hayden shouted. The sounds of the gasps and the footsteps were nearing again, and no doubt the zombies would soon be in sight. "We need as much help as anyone. Everyone needs help. But we don't get help anymore. And we don't get *to* help. We ... we just have to help ourselves."

Clarice narrowed her tearful eyes. That judgemental scowl Hayden had seen so many times, more so in his twenties than when they were kids, covered her face. "Maybe you don't think you have to help. But you don't make my decisions for me."

Before Hayden could protest, she ran back into the cul-de-sac they'd just escaped from.

"Oh for fuck's ..."

He saw a man on his own. He was in the middle of one of the gardens. He looked of Asian descent, and was wearing a green coat and blue jeans. He had dark hair and brown eyes. Looked like he was usually well-maintained.

Usually, because right now there were two zombies closing in on him, getting ready to bite.

Clarice was running towards them with the gun raised.

"Jesus Christ, Sis," Hayden said. He ran in her direction. Tried not to look down the road where the bigger group of zombies were coming for them. This was suicide. Maniacal suicide.

The things you do for family.

The man struggled and shouted out as the two zombies snapped at him. "Please! I—I don't wanna—I don't wanna—"

Clarice raised the gun higher. Slowed down. Pointed it at the zombies.

"Put it down, Sis," he said. "You'll take the poor guy's head off."

Hayden rushed past his sister and swung the axe straight into the mouth of the first zombie. He heard bone crack as the zombie's head flew back, and cold blood spilled out of the bottom of its chin.

"Argghhh!"

The second zombie had the Asian guy on the ground.

Teeth were wrapping around the side of his chest.

Hayden steadied his grip.

Swung the axe at the back of the zombie's neck.

The zombie shook, went into spasm, and then went completely rigid and fell on top of the Asian guy, blood pooling out of it. A clean shot.

"Come the hell on," Hayden said, holding a hand out for the Asian guy.

The guy muttered inaudible words. He put his hands together. "Thank you. Thank you so much. Thank you so much."

Hayden grabbed the top of his coat and pulled him up. Just along the road, he could see the zombies approaching. At least fifty of them, all piling down the road. "We need to get out of here or you'll have nothing to thank me for, believe me."

The guy's pupils looked dilated, like he'd literally stepped onto the brink of death and only a part of him had come back. "I—I—"

"Come on!" Clarice shouted, and Hayden was instantly impressed by his sister's assertiveness.

The guy shook and jumped and then he saw the zombies coming down the road. "Shit. Oh shit. Oh shit."

"You can 'oh shit' all you want when we get the hell off this road," Hayden said, dragging the guy along, his sister aiding him. "Riversford Industrial Estate. You know it?"

The guy's pace seemed to pick up in an instant upon hearing those words. "I ... I—"

"Do you know it and can you take us there?"

Hayden looked at the guy as they ran out of the top of the cul-de-sac once more, the zombies edging closer to their prey.

He looked back at Hayden and smiled shakily. "I know it. And I can take you there. Is it—is there something there? Some kind of—of shelter? 'Cause I heard a few rumours but I'm not sure if—"

"That's what we're trying to find out," Hayden said. "Now let's get out of here."

The three of them took a right on "Manish's" directions, and they followed the trees at the side of the road, the ever-constant hum of the zombies following behind them.

IF HE'D PAID MORE attention, and if Clarice had paid more attention, they'd have seen exactly what was watching them from the opposite side of the road.

What was edging closer.

And maybe if they had, things would've worked out different.

TWENTY-TWO

Hayden, Clarice and Manish finally collapsed after a good twenty minutes of running.

They sat at the side of the road and leaned back against a brick wall. Sweat poured down Hayden's face, and it was so cold that it just made him feel even worse. His heart felt like it was going to burst through his chest, and his hand was wrapped so tightly around the axe that it felt numb.

"Riversford," Clarice said, panting what must've been her billionth breath today. "It's ... it's near here?"

Manish nodded. He wasn't panting as badly. There was still a detachment about him. A detachment that Hayden wasn't sure he liked. Admittedly, he'd nearly been savaged by zombies, but he seemed to be calm. Coping better than any of them.

Then again, wouldn't every stranger seem suspicious after their luck with strangers so far?

"It's about a mile up the road from here," Manish said. "It—it's a big place. Covers a lot of land. Few hangars in there. Dunno how—how they're supposed to be keeping the flesh eaters out."

"That's what we're hoping to find out," Hayden said. And then the reality of the situation dawned on him. It was the first time he'd had a chance to properly catch his breath since Newbie's death. The whole reason they'd come to Warrington in the first place was to find Newbie's daughter. Sure, there was the lure of the safe place that Newbie's transmission picked up, but Hayden was never too sure about that.

But the whole question of his being here struck him hard right now: why was he here? Why was his sister here?

Manish must've been reading his mind. "You—you don't sound like you're from around here."

Hayden scanned Manish's face. He had a few lines on his forehead, but his face was relatively young looking. Probably in his thirties, or even his late twenties, it was hard to say. He looked at Hayden in the same way Hayden probably looked at him—with distrust, with curiosity. Looked like he'd had a rough time on the road himself.

Which always brought questions along with it. How had he made it this far? Who else was he surviving with?

What were his secrets? Because everyone had secrets.

"We're from Smileston," Clarice said, breaking the silence. The road was still and completely quiet. There were no houses around, and the sounds of the groaning zombies were gone. They'd come, of course. Follow them until they caught them. Or maybe they'd get distracted. Find somebody else to hunt down and feast on.

Hayden felt terrible for even considering that diversion a better option.

"Smilestown?" Manish said. "I—I've never even heard of Smiles—"

"Smileston," Hayden said. Always got on his nerves how people mispronounced his hometown. "We came a long way because we heard there was somewhere in Warrington. Somewhere letting people in to start again. You not from around here, either?"

Manish lowered his head. He rubbed his hands against his jeans. "I—I'm from Appleton. Just south of here."

"And how've you made it this far?"

"What?"

"How are you alive? How have you made it this far?"

Manish opened his shaky mouth like he was about to respond. And then he closed it. Sighed. Hayden could smell he had bad breath—like everyone in the post-tooth brushing age. "How have any of us made it this far?"

It was a fair point.

They stood up and walked slowly along the brick wall at the side of the road. Through the hedges across the street, Hayden could see the grey metal of a looming industrial site, and he knew exactly where it was. Riversford. Their destination. Their glimmer of hope.

A dim, fading glimmer of hope, but a glimmer of hope nonetheless.

"I'm guessing it's ... it's just as bad in Smiles ... Smileston?"

Clarice nodded. "If not worse. Our place got bombed."

"You got the jets? Then you were the lucky ones."

"What do you mean?" Hayden asked.

Manish shook his head to dismiss the comment, but when he saw Hayden was still glaring at him, he probably figured he wasn't going to be allowed to let that one drop. "I ... Sometimes I think it would've been better if the jets had just flown over Appleton and bombed the place. While I was still asleep. Before—before all this mess. Because then I wouldn't have had to get chased like I was back there. I wouldn't have had to see the things I've seen. Or ..."

He let that one go.

Hayden didn't press him. He kind of knew what he was going to say.

Or do the things I've done.

"Don't you ever feel that way?" Manish asked. "Like—like just giving up? Because this is hell, surely. Only it's a forgiving kind of hell 'cause there's still the chance of opting out. But then sometimes I wonder if this is just ... just the prelude to the burning. That if I opt out, my god will punish me. Like this is all some kind of-of test. But I don't know what I've done to deserve it. I don't know what I've done."

"None of us have done anything to deserve it," Clarice said. But Hayden couldn't agree with her. Not exactly. He'd been a shitty brother and a shitty son in the years building up to the fall of society. He'd pulled himself away from his friends, distanced himself from his loving family who'd done everything for him when he was growing up. Even when his older sister killed herself when Hayden was only in high school, they'd kept on doing everything.

And all Hayden had been was an ungrateful bastard.

He'd deserved it.

"What's your story, then?" Hayden asked.

Manish picked some loose skin from the corners of his well-bitten nails as they walked. "I—I woke up and people were killing each other in the streets. I thought at first there was some kind of —of war. Some extremist group or another finally uprising. And that terrified me. But—but then I saw the dead coming back to life at the masjid near my house. I saw people I knew—friends, good people—being bitten and then ... and then coming back to life." His voice quivered, and he shook his head. "It was awful. The worst thing I've ever witnessed."

"I can relate to that," Hayden said. He looked at Clarice. "We both can. We ... we've both lost people we knew. People we care about."

"My sympathies," Manish said, turning from Hayden to Clarice and then back at Hayden again.

Hayden couldn't avoid the twinge of ill-feeling in his stomach when Manish laid eyes on his sister.

A twinge of protectiveness.

A protectiveness that had always been there.

"What about after?" Hayden asked.

"After what?"

"You say you locked yourself in your house in Appleton and now you're up here in Warrington. What brought you here?"

Hayden was trying—and he only realised this right now—to catch Manish out. To find a kink in his story. Because there was something strange about him. Something ... off. He just couldn't put his finger on what it was.

But Manish replied with a perfectly respectable answer. "I came here for the same reason anyone goes anywhere these days: family."

"And did you find your family?" Clarice asked.

Manish didn't look at Clarice this time. Instead, he looked at Hayden in a way that made goose pimples rise up his arms. "I think so," he said.

Hayden was about to question Manish some more when Manish stopped walking and pointed up ahead.

"Do you see them?" he asked.

Hayden squinted ahead. "See what?"

"The people. On the roof of that hangar. There ... there are people there."

"Shit," Clarice said. "So it's for real."

It took Hayden a few seconds to pinpoint exactly where the other two were looking, but eventually he saw it clearly. On top of a metal industrial hangar—some postal depot by the looks of things—there were a group of people. Hayden could count three, but there might've been more. They were all looking out into the distance.

Looking out, like they were trying to find something.

Someone.

Manish walked ahead. "Thank you so much, again. Truly. We must go there now. We must—"

"We need to scout it out first. See if anyone else goes inside. I still ... I still don't have a great feeling. About this place."

Manish sighed and shook his head.

Clarice tutted. "Believe me, he's always like this," she said.

And then she turned and looked at Hayden with her twinkling blue eyes, smiled at him like she smiled at him when he encouraged her as a kid, when he told her to stand up to bullies and when he gave her a chocolate from his secret stash.

"You need to learn to tr—"

Clarice didn't finish speaking.

Something whooshed from behind them.

Blood spurted out of her chest.

And then she fell to her knees and smacked her head against the concrete, the life drifting out of her ever-colourful eyes.

TWENTY-THREE

Hayden watched his sister tumble to the ground, the sound of gunfire still echoing in his ears.

He didn't have time to think about who was firing at them. He didn't have time to worry about them. He didn't even have time to think about running away.

Because all he cared about was on the road, bleeding from just above her chest.

The one thing he'd sworn to protect—the one person left in his life that he actually gave a real shit about—was on the concrete, her eyes closing.

"Hayden, we—we need to run!"

Hayden heard Manish's voice somewhere to his right but it was distant, echoey, out of focus. He rushed over to Clarice's body as she lay on the concrete. The camouflage jacket she was wearing had split at the back where the bullet had hit her. To his left, Hayden could hear voices, and a car gradually approaching.

But he crouched down at Clarice's side and put a hand on her back, prayed to God she was okay, prayed to God she wouldn't die, not now, not after how far they'd come.

"Sis, please," Hayden said. He didn't know what else to say. He had a hand on her wrist but his hands were shaking so much that he couldn't tell if there was a pulse or not. He thought he could feel her breathing against his hand but maybe that was just his own breath. He couldn't tell. He didn't know.

So he just kept a hand on Clarice's back and let the warm tears roll down his cheeks as the voices and the engine got closer.

"I'd stay on the fucking ground if I were you, sunshine," a gruff, almost Scottish sounding man said. "Unless you wanna end up like your girlfriend."

Hayden felt a burning sensation cripple his chest. He pulled the gun out of Clarice's pocket. Tensed his fingers around it. Stood up, held his breath, turned and pointed at the group coming his way, not caring what happened to him anymore, only caring about avenging his sister, making the fuckers pay for what they'd done to her.

But when he turned to face the group, he noticed something. Three things, in fact.

First off was the car. A black Range Rover incredibly similar to the one he'd stolen from the cottage that had broken down on the road to Warrington.

And then there was the woman. Sammy. The woman with the ginger hair who Hayden had held a gun to the head of. She was looking at Hayden with wide-eyed fear, with a distance and detachment that made it look like she almost regretted being here in her present company.

But most interesting of all was the third thing he saw.

The person he saw, a black guy standing behind her, a gun to her head.

Sarah.

"You're gonna wanna drop that," the gruff-voiced guy said again. He was narrow-faced, had shortish dark hair and was wearing a leather jacket that looked way too new and unmarked to have been his for long. "Unless you wanna get another innocent person's blood on your hands, I'd lower that gun."

Hayden looked into Sarah's eyes. There were no tears there, just recognition. She had bruises on her cheeks and cuts on the top of her head. She looked like she'd been through a rough time.

But she was alive. She'd survived.

"Hey. You hear me? Drop that gun."

Hayden blinked and looked away from Sarah. It didn't seem like the group knew that Hayden and Sarah had anything to do with one another, and judging by how they were using her as leverage as it was, Hayden wanted to keep it that way.

He held the gun towards the gruff guy, who pointed a long black hunting rifle in his direction. Hayden's finger shook on the trigger. He wanted to fire it. Fire it right into the guy's neck and send a shower of blood spurting out of his jugular. He wanted to destroy him for what he'd done to Clarice.

But he held his breath. Let his pulse pound through his skull. Lowered his gun.

The gruff-voiced guy smiled. "Good. Good. Now drop onto your knees like your rag-head friend and slide that gun over here."

Hayden didn't know what the racist wanker was referring to at first, and then he looked and saw Manish on his knees with his hands on the back of his head. He was shivering, and Hayden could hear his anxious breathing from here. The smell of urine was filling the air.

"Get down. Or I'll pop another cap into your girlfriend's head to make sure she's dead."

"She's my sister," Hayden shouted. "She ... she's my little sister. And she did—she did nothing to hurt you."

The gruff-voiced guy raised his eyebrows. "Oh. Is that so? See I've been hearing things differently. I've been hearing that you and that bird and some nigger who ain't with you anymore all seemed awful happy to raid that cottage back north. Ain't that right, Sam?"

Sammy swallowed heavily. She lowered her eyes so she wasn't looking directly at Hayden and she nodded.

"And what if we did?" Hayden said. He kept his gun in his hand. Stayed on his feet. A clock ticked inside his head. A countdown of how long his sister had left. She had to get medical treatment. Some kind of professional help. She had to get to the safe haven—fast.

The gruff-voiced guy smiled even wider and shook his head. "Look, I'm gonna make this extra clear to you cause you don't seem to be all too wise about it right now. Your cute wee sis is dying on the road there. And she's gonna bleed out if you keep on being a stubborn fucker. And we ain't got no problem with that. You killed one of ours; we kill one of yours. Sounds even. But we ain't nasty fuckers. We reason. We understand why people do what they do. But there's gonna be no understandin' if you don't put your gun on the ground and get onto your fucking knees, pal."

Hayden kept hold of the gun but his grip was loosening. The words, the reality, hit him hard. Clarice was on the road. She was dying. She needed help.

Clarice. His little sister.

He couldn't lose her. No matter what that meant, he just couldn't lose her.

He took a deep breath of the cool air and threw the pistol a few feet ahead of him. It was only then that he saw his axe was already on the road. Must've dropped it when Clarice got shot.

He got down onto his knees and he felt a warmth seep through his legs.

He looked down and realised it was Clarice's blood.

He felt tears filling up in his eyes as he crouched in her blood. She hadn't said a word. Hadn't moved a muscle. It didn't bode well. He didn't know where exactly she'd been shot, what it meant. But he couldn't bear to look at her. He couldn't bring himself to look at his baby sister on the road like that.

"I'm here, Clarice. Your big brother's here. I promise."

The black guy threw Sarah into the back of the Range Rover. Sammy climbed into the back seat. The two men—gruff voiced guy and silent black guy—marched in Hayden, Clarice and Manish's direction looking awfully proud of themselves.

The gruff-voiced guy pressed the rifle right underneath Hayden's chin, stuffed the barrel right into his Adam's apple. He peered at Hayden with nasty eyes. Bully eyes. Eyes that Hayden imagined when he pictured what his older sister Annabelle went through when she was younger.

Cruel eyes.

"You care an awful lot about your sister," the guy said, pulling Hayden's head up even higher as the black guy lifted Clarice over his shoulder and walked her back to the car. Hayden had to use all the resistance he had to avoid following him, to avoid twitching.

Keep calm or your head's coming off, keep calm, keep calm.

"Wouldn't you?" Hayden said.

The gruff-voiced guy's smile got wider; his eyes got even more bloodshot, nasty, excited. "Oh no, I wasn't criticising you. It's a good thing."

He pulled the barrel of the gun to the side and held it back like a club.

"The more you care about her, the more fun we're gonna have with you."

And then he swung the gun against Hayden's face and Hayden felt something crack.

TWENTY-FOUR

Hayden crouched in complete darkness as the Range Rover sped down the road, getting closer and closer to the Riversford Industrial Estate, closer and closer to the supposed safe place.

The left side of his face stung. Every time he squinted at the light peeking through the trees outside, he felt a sharp pain spread right around his head. He swore the gruff-voiced guy—who's name he'd now overhead as Ally—had broken something. He swore he'd done some serious damage.

But that was the least of his concerns right now. His major concern was Clarice. How long she had left—if she had any time left at all.

And what he'd do to Ally if she died.

The things he'd die himself to do to Ally given the opportunity.

He was stuffed in the back of the Range Rover in a cage that was barely big enough to fit a dog, let alone three people. Sarah was in there with him, dirty white gag wrapped around her mouth. Manish was in there too, but he couldn't stop whimpering, couldn't stop crying. Hayden wondered how the hell a guy as soft as him had made it this far, but then again he remembered himself just a week ago. Scared. Terrified, even. Convinced death was imminent—which it still was.

But he'd just grown more confident. He'd adapted to the new world. And yes, it took it out of him. Yes, he had to change every day, every minute, every hour to keep up with the rules of this new place. But he was doing okay. He was alive.

Until now, anyway. Because his sister was all that he was living for.

"We're gonna get out of this," Hayden said, as the Range Rover bounced over potholes in the road, sending his tender head slamming against the top of the cage. "We ... we're going to find a way out somehow. And we're—"

"But what's the point of—of even getting out if your sister needs help?" Manish muttered through his sobs and tears.

He had a point, too. A point that was dwelling on Hayden's exhausted mind. What *was* the point of escaping their current situation—for him, at least? Because his sister needed help. Serious medical help. And all running away was, was running away from her.

He couldn't run away from her.

"You ... you should find a way out," Hayden said. "Both of you. You don't need to be here."

Sarah mumbled something under her gag. Something that Hayden couldn't make out, but it sounded like a noise of disagreement.

"I ... I should probably be honest," Manish said. "I'm—I'm not good. On my own. I've—I've been with three groups. Since—since all this horrible stuff started. And I ..." He stopped speaking, sniffed back some more tears. "The last group I was with. Nice people. But—but we were staying in a cabin just inside Warrington for a night. I was on watch. And—and I saw them coming. Saw the flesh eaters coming. And I wanted to let the others in the group know. Believe me, I wanted that. But I just ... I saw an opportunity. An opportunity to get out and—and to use the others, the live ones, as a distraction. So I ran. I took a crowbar and some food and I ran."

He descended into more guilty sobs.

"I ... I'll never forget their screams as I ran away. And—and the voice. A woman called Harriet. The last thing she said —'Where the fuck's Manish?' And that just ... that just broke me. Because she wasn't saying it accusationally. She was genuinely worried. Worried about me. And I'd just left them. And—and by then it was too late to do anything. I was on my own."

Another smack to the head as the Range Rover went over a bump in the road, then swung to the left.

Hayden understood what Manish was saying. And the strangest part about it all was how numb he felt about the words. It was like they were irrelevant somehow. Like the weight of what Manish had done—the guilt it was pressing down on his shoulders —was minimal.

"You did what you had to do to survive," Hayden said. "Anyone in your shoes would've done the exact same."

Although it was pitch black, Hayden got the sense that Manish was looking at him in the darkness, as his short, shaky breaths cut through the silence. "Do—do you mean that?"

Hayden went to reply and then the right side of his face flew into the grating on the cage.

The Range Rover stopped. The engine cut out.

He heard a door open at the side. Heard muffled voices outside—voices he didn't recognise. He tensed his fists. Readied himself for whatever was coming. He had no idea whether he was going to have to fight or scrap or whether Ally and his friends were just going to pop a bullet in his head and ditch him on the side of the road for zombie-feed.

The boot opened up with a creak. Light filled the cage.

At the other side, Ally stood with a smile on his face.

He unclipped the cage then pointed his gun at the three of them in the back again. "Come on," he said. "Time for you to meet the boss."

TWENTY-FIVE

When Ally dragged Hayden out of the back of the Range Rover, he knew right away that his bad feeling about Riversford might just be right.

The place looked empty. Void of life, not like his hopes and dreams had made it out to be—bustling, full of positivity, optimism, hope.

Just a wide, empty parking area, waterlogged grey stones. People stood on top of the large metal industrial hangars holding guns and looking down at them as Hayden, Manish and Sarah were pushed across the concrete by Ally, Sammy and a ginger guy that Hayden hadn't seen before.

There were high fences all around the outskirts of Riversford. Decent for keeping zombies out. But the sheer lack of life in this place was haunting. There was no sign of men, women, children all surviving in here. Just men with guns, the glimmer of movement in some of the hangar windows.

"Get a fucking move on," Ally said. He pushed the barrel of the gun right into the bottom of Hayden's spine, knocked the wind out of him.

"My sister," Hayden said, looking around the grounds and trying to find her. "Where's—"

"Don't worry yourself about your sister," Ally said. "Bob's taken her to get medical treatment. Told you we were the warm, loving type."

He laughed, and Hayden couldn't argue. They hardly came across as warm and fluffy, that was for sure.

They walked across the grounds, went past a huge stack of petrol canisters and to a blue-painted garage at the sides of one of the hangars. It had *CityFast Parcel Depot* on the side of it. Hayden figured any other visit here would be a good time to lambast City-Fast for the shitty experience he'd had when having things delivered with them, but those times had passed. He had bigger problems on his plate right now.

He longed for the times when his biggest drama of the week was whether he was going to get his new video game through on a Monday or a Tuesday.

They walked through the hangar entrance. There was a chubby-faced guy stood there wearing a wooly green CityFast fleece and blue jeans, holding a gun. He nodded at Ally as he entered, and Ally nodded right back at him. It wasn't the most comfortable exchange. There was something stilted about it. Much like the way Sammy didn't seem comfortable in Ally's presence, there was a forced nature to the exchanges between these people.

A secret.

"Now when we get upstairs, I expect you guys to be on your best behaviour. The boss has enough aggro to deal with without you three makin' it worse." He prodded the gun further into Hayden's back. "And when he finds out what you did to Dave, well ... Things ain't gonna be pretty."

He laughed, and it made the hairs on Hayden's arms stand.

Ally, Sammy and the other guy pushed the trio through a reception area and towards a narrow flight of concrete steps.

Hayden looked up them and held his breath. It smelled weird in here, like damp and sweat. There was a sourness to the air too. A sourness that made him feel queasy. A sourness he couldn't quite comprehend, but which gave him an undeniable bad feeling.

"Come on," Ally said.

He prodded the gun further into Hayden's back, and Hayden was forced to climb.

Every step Hayden took, he felt like a prisoner walking to the gallows to be executed. And maybe because that was happening—maybe he was just a prisoner. Maybe they were going to strap a jumpsuit on him so this "boss" could find justice after Hayden killing Dave.

They climbed slowly. Hayden's footsteps echoed against the dusty concrete steps. His mouth dried.

When they reached the top of the stairs, the place seemed to lighten up. Which was a pleasant surprise, since Hayden had it in his mind that he'd be heading to some pitch black gas chamber disguised as a shower room or something.

"Take a right," Ally said.

Hayden turned right and he was surprised to see a man sitting at a desk jotting away on a pad of paper.

There was a huge glass window behind him. A window that looked right out over the surrounding houses and countryside. The structures of the town of Warrington were visible in the distance.

Hayden's footsteps echoed on the solid floor as he was pushed towards the guy. And the more he was pushed, the more he started to suspect that this guy was the "boss." But he wasn't anything like Hayden expected. He had thinning white hair, with thick-rimmed glasses perched on the edge of his nose. He was wearing a loose-necked black cardigan, with light brown corduroy trousers—trousers that were too short, exposing his hobbly, bare ankles.

And he just kept focused on the notepad. Kept on scribbling away. Didn't once look up.

When they were just a few feet from the desk, Ally grabbed Hayden's back and told him to stop. Manish and Sarah stopped too, their feet squeaking against the tiles.

And still, this man didn't lift his head.

It was a few seconds before Ally cleared his throat and broke the silence. "Boss. Got three for you. Taken one of 'em down to medical bay. A woman. She ... she got shot in crossfire. But this one here, he killed Dave. Sammy here saw it with her own eyes. Didn't you, Sam?"

Sammy nodded. Hayden could see that her cheeks were going red, her eyes were watering. She kept her wide eyes off the Boss. A far cry from the seemingly strong woman who Hayden had held a gun to the head of back at the cottage.

Boss stopped scribbling. He clicked the button on his pen, pulled his glasses onto the top of his head, and then he looked up at Hayden, Manish and Sarah. He half-smiled at them with his thin little mouth, then looked at them all in turn, intently. He didn't speak. Nobody spoke. The only sound was of Hayden's heart thumping, of Sammy's feet shuffling against the dusty floor.

Finally, Boss broke the silence. He squeaked his chair back and stood up. He was shorter than Hayden expected. Definitely only clocked in at five nine. But there was something intimidating about him, clearly. Something that scared Sammy—something that scared all of them. Hayden could just see it in their expressions, hear it in their voices.

This man had something on them.

Hayden didn't want to know what.

He held a hand out and it took a few seconds for Hayden to realise he was offering it to shake. "Callum Hessenthaler," he said.

Hayden didn't want to take his hand, but he had to. He had to play it cool if he wanted any chance of his sister surviving. He wondered where she was. How she was. He hoped to God she was okay.

He took Callum's hand and shook. There was no strength to his grip, and his palm felt as greasy as an eel's back. Callum fast pulled it away, and shook Manish's hand.

He didn't even look at Sarah.

"So, go on then," Callum said, like a bemused teacher waiting to hear why one kid had another in a headlock. "What happened with Dave?"

It was a direct question that Hayden wasn't expecting. "We ... I didn't mean to—"

"Just tell me. Straight up. No time for nonsense in this world."

Again, the directness of the guy startled Hayden. He'd been expecting a boss of this place to be full of grandiose speeches about why it was safe, why it was the place to be, that kind of thing. But Callum was direct. Straight up. A man who seemingly practiced what he preached.

Hayden replayed the events as he remembered them. "I ... We went into the cottage to find some food. We just needed a vehicle. But we were heading here. We were heading to this place. We heard the transmission and ... and Newbie wondered if maybe his kid was here." Hayden wanted to spill everything out at once. Newbie's death. The standoff at the cottage. Clarice being shot.

But then Callum interrupted.

"I'm assuming Newbie isn't with you anymore?"

Hayden thought back to the sight of Newbie's body sprawled out on the driveway outside his house. He shook his head. "No, he—"

"Surname?"

"Erm ... Pearce. I think. His wife left a note. A note saying they were heading here. His ... his daughter was called Amy."

It struck Hayden then how strange it was that this place should be so quiet, so empty, if people had actually left for it. Had people just not made it here? Surely *some* people had made it, beyond the gun-toting nutters who he'd seen up to now?

Callum half-smiled. His lips were dry and cracked. "I can investigate into that for you."

He walked back around the desk and pulled out his chair.

"Where ... where is everyone around here?" Hayden asked. "Families, and ...?"

Callum picked up his pen and clicked the top of it again. He looked up at Hayden as if he'd only half heard him.

But there was a new kind of look on his face this time.

A different kind of twinkle to his eyes.

"Ally, Gav, why don't you show them where the families around here are?" he said. He opened his drawer and threw a key to Ally.

Ally sniggered. The guard called Gav let out a little laugh. Sammy's cheeks went redder. Something was wrong. This whole exchange was just wrong.

"I need to see my sister," Hayden said.

And then he felt the gun against his back again. He felt Ally grab hold of him, drag him back.

Callum smiled. "Oh you will. She'll be just fine here. Promise."

And then he looked at Sarah and Sammy.

"You two stay. I want a word with you, Sam. And with this new girl here."

"She comes with us," Hayden said, struggling.

"Why?" Callum asked. His eyes split through Hayden. "Do you know her or something? I'll take the expression on your face as a 'yes'."

Fuck. He didn't want to give that one away. And by the way Ally whooped, he'd really dropped himself—and Sarah—into it even more.

"Got an extra one of your lot!" he said, as he dragged Hayden back, his grip sending stinging pains right through his arms. "Even better."

Hayden tried to fight back, tried to shout out, but before he knew it he had a damp-tasting gag around his mouth and all he could do was mumble.

"Don't be alarmed," Callum said, as Gav and Ally dragged Manish and him further away. "We're going to take extra special care of your sister. I promise you that."

Hayden saw the fear on Sammy's face as she looked back at him.

He saw Sarah getting further away.

And then he turned the stairs and he saw nothing but the grey concrete walls again.

But as he struggled and shook to get from out of Ally's grip, it was the look on Sammy's face when Callum mentioned Hayden's sister that terrified him the most.

A look of pure, pale-faced dread.

TWENTY-SIX

Callum Hessenthaler had been hoping for a good session on his work-in-progress before that goon Ally Chester came storming in.

He was working on a non-fiction book. Well, partly non-fiction: there were elements of it that were fictional too. It was about a fictional man's survival in a post-apocalyptic world, and how society reacts to the challenges it has posed to it.

But the experiences he documented were real. Very real.

He just had to hope his pad didn't get damaged anytime soon.

And now Sammy Harrison and some other new woman were in his office area. He could smell the sweat coming off both of them and it was disgusting. They needed a wash. A proper shower.

They had a duty. A role to fulfill. They couldn't fulfill that role smelling like this.

"Sammy, what happened back there? At the cottage?"

Sammy tilted her head in that pathetic way she always did. The way she'd done when she first got here, when they found her out in the open wandering through the streets with her two children. The streets Callum's people had *saved* her from.

Ungrateful behaviour she'd displayed since, really. Not the kind of behaviour you expect from someone in her position.

"I ... I tried to stop him but it was just—"

"You didn't try hard enough," Callum said. He got up from the leather office chair. Walked over to Sammy, keeping a smile on his face regardless of the bubbling frustration within. The other woman—the gagged woman with the bruised eye and the brown hair—was completely quiet. Callum could see the fear drifting into her face. It wasn't ideal. He didn't want people to fear him.

He just wanted people to *understand* him.

Or specifically, he wanted women to understand him.

He stopped opposite Sammy. Reached for her chin and lifted her head. She was tall. Or at least, as tall as him, which admittedly wasn't all that tall after all.

He looked into her crystal-like eyes and he saw nothing but misery, nothing but fear. "Do you want to see your children again? Your Renate and your Sebastian?"

Her eyes lit up with hope. That was nice. Hope was nice. Everyone needed a little hope in this world.

"Then turn around. Look over by the stairs. Look who's coming to see you."

Sammy frowned. Her cheeks flushed. She turned and looked over her shoulder.

And that's when Callum Hessenthaler held his breath and grabbed the long, sharp razor from the edge of his desk and wrapped a hand around Sammy's mouth, pulled her back, pressed the razor blade deep into her neck and slit.

He listened to her mumble and cry out as blood spurted out of her neck all over the dusty floor. The gagged woman looked on in wide-eyed horror as Sammy twitched, shook, convulsed. As warm, thick streams of blood splattered down her front and covered Callum's hand.

"I'm sorry. You hush now. You're nearly with your children."

He held Sammy's mouth and waited for the blood flow to ease, waited for her mumbled screams to stop.

He didn't like killing people.

He didn't want to have to kill Sammy.

But she'd misbehaved. He'd trusted her, and she'd stepped out of place.

And this is what happened when people stepped out of place.

He gently lay her body down on the floor and he turned to the gagged woman.

Blood dripped from the razor and onto the dusty floor and fear sparkled in her striking blue eyes.

TWENTY-SEVEN

Hayden knew something was wrong the second he caught a whiff of the smell.

Ally pushed him in through a rusty metal door at the back of the *CityFast* hangar, which he'd unlocked with a similarly rusty key dangling on a chain. He still had that gun wedged in Hayden's spine, and it was growing more painful by the minute. He could hear Manish whimpering as Gav eased him in through the door, in towards the darkness, the smell.

Hayden wanted to shout out, but he knew it was worthless. There was nobody here who could help them. And all shouting out would do was attract zombies to their location.

He didn't have a gag wrapped around his mouth, but he might as well have done. He understood that, everyone understood that.

"You're gonna move where we push you," Ally said, his voice echoing against the narrow walls. There was a chill to this corridor, and that horrible smell—urine, sweat, faeces. All of them mixed in a horrible cocktail that made the hairs stand up on Hayden's arms; made him wonder what he was going to find. "Any wrong move, you're gettin' a bullet in your back, sunshine."

Gav mumbled something in Manish's ear and, judging by Manish's shivery breath, it couldn't have been good.

Hayden followed the push of Ally's gun and moved through the narrow corridors. When the door had closed, it went completely dark. There was a dampness underfoot that Hayden could feel seeping through the broken tips of his shoes. And somewhere ahead, somewhere in the distance and down the corridor, he could hear something.

A kind of … mumbling.

"Had a bet with Bob you're gonna like what you see. Might be a shock to the system at first—shock to the old ways and all that —but you'll come round. We always do come round. Or we die."

Ally jabbed the gun further into Hayden's back. Hayden wanted to turn around and punch the bastard, but he knew that would be no use. His sister was being treated somewhere. Sarah was with the boss, Callum, and that ginger woman, Sammy.

There was something wrong about all of this. The fear on Sammy's face, and on the faces of a handful of guards Hayden had seen around this place since. There was some kind of unspoken secret. An unspoken secret that Hayden felt himself getting closer and closer to unearthing.

"Take a right," Ally said, a flicker of spit hitting Hayden's left ear. "And remember, no—"

"I'm not going anywhere until I know my sister is being looked after. Don't worry."

He heard a snigger from Gav. And then he felt Ally's breaths get more frequent on his ear, on the back of his neck.

"Oh she's being looked after alright," Ally said.

He said it with just enough sincerity to puzzle Hayden.

Was he being serious? Was she actually being cared for? Or was something else going on here?

All signs pointed to the latter. Everything in Hayden's mind screamed at him to do something, to save his sister from this place, to get the hell out of here.

But what could he do, really?

They took a right and at the end of the current corridor, Hayden saw a glimmer of light.

It peeked through the bars of a metal door just ahead. The smell got stronger as they approached, and the water under his feet deepened, pooling into his shoes and freezing his toes. As he walked towards the door, he wasn't sure he wanted to see what was inside.

And then he heard the whimpering.

"Please. Please. Please—please don't."

He didn't recognise the voice but it sent another cold shiver through his body. It was a woman's voice. Undeniably a woman's voice. And judging by the lack of women Hayden had seen around here—Sammy aside, and she was hardly enthusiastic about her duties—it didn't take a genius to figure out what might be going on.

They stopped right in front of the door. Hayden's heart pounded in his chest as Ally reached around the back of him and unlocked the door. He looked at Hayden; his sweaty, bearded face lit up in the glimmer of light. He smiled, revealing his yellow, coffee and cigarette stained teeth. "Just hold your breath. Gonna be a bit of a shock to the system. But you'll get used to it."

And then he lowered the squeaky handle and pushed open the door.

When the door opened, Hayden didn't understand what he was looking at. He could see where the light was coming from now—a small candle in a glass lantern flickering orange light around the dim, grey room.

And then he saw the hair.

He saw the dark, greasy hair of a woman. She was chained up to the wall by her neck. She was completely naked, covered in sweat. Her face was puffed up with bruises. Scratches and scars lined her inner thighs.

She looked up at Hayden as he stepped through the door, but

he couldn't see beyond her swollen eyelids. He could just see the fluid of a beating that looked like glimmering tears. He could just see a loss of humanity. Dehumanisation.

His body tensed. He wanted to run. He wanted to help this poor woman, bound by her neck, arms and ankles, and he wanted to get away.

But when he backed into the sharp barrel of Ally's gun, he saw something else.

There was another woman beside her. A black woman with frizzy hair, also naked, also bound, also beaten.

And then there was another woman—a chubby woman with greying hair.

A skinny woman of eastern descent.

Hayden looked around at this room of horrors, heart racing, nausea welling in his chest, building up in his stomach.

"If the world's gonna survive, we need two things: to breed, and to fuck," Ally said. He grinned, and a little laugh came out of Gav's mouth. "And you can't have the breedin' without the fuckin'!"

TWENTY-EIGHT

Hayden couldn't stop the vomit from creeping up his throat and spurting out of his mouth.

He spewed up all over the floor, which was already wet with pools of urine, sweat, blood and other stuff. He could hear the chains of the tied up women in the room ahead of him rattling as they mumbled and cried out underneath their gags.

Women. Lots of women. All of them tied up for one purpose —to serve the urges of the sick bastards in charge of the Riversford Industrial Estate.

Ally laughed when Hayden threw up and patted his back. "Told you it'd be a shock to the damned system, didn't I? How's the raghead copin', Gaz, huh? He pukin' too?"

Manish was just staring ahead at the room of women, the whites of his eyes bulging in the darkness. His bottom lip was shaking, and tears rolled down his cheeks. A pure look of shock, of hopelessness, covered him.

"Makes a kind of sense though, huh?" Ally said, turning back to Hayden. "I mean, the world's dying. And when a world's dying, women ain't all too keen on breeding. So the least we can do is enforce it. I mean, we're gonna need kids. The new world's gonna need kids. Otherwise what's the point? We can't just let the world die. Can't just let it rot away. Huh?"

Hayden's eyes burned as he stared at the chained up women. He felt bad even looking at them. He felt like he was contributing to their degradation by standing here and not doing a thing.

"Like I said, we're gonna look after your sister. We'll go easy on her. Although I've gotta say, she's a pretty girl, so maybe you'll let us off if we go a bit rough."

Hayden couldn't control himself.

A switch inside him flipped.

He swung around and smacked Ally's head against the side of the alley wall. He heard the gun blast, felt his ears ringing, but he wasn't hurting so it couldn't have shot him, he was okay, he was fine.

He pushed Ally onto the ground and he grabbed his wrist, tried to pry the gun from him, tried to yank it out of his hand and shove it into his mouth and blow his brains out for even suggesting what he was going to do to Clarice.

But then he felt something press against the right side of his head.

"Don't move another muscle," Gaz said. "Or I'll blow your frigging brains out."

Hayden kept tight hold of Ally's wrist. Ally was struggling and tensing, but that god-awful smile was still spread across his face. Like this was all some kind of joke, some sick game.

"They're ... they're people," Hayden said. "People with feelings. With emotions."

"Emotions get you killed," Ally said. "Just like they're gonna get you and your friend killed if you don't get the hell off me right this second."

Hayden felt the gun move from his head then back to his head again, Gaz clearly struggling to keep tabs on Manish and Hayden at the same time. Hayden kept on holding onto Ally's wrist. He could yank the gun from his hands. Blow his brains out and end this, right here.

He could rescue those women, rescue his sister, get the hell out of here.

"Y'know, when you mentioned that mate of yours, Newbie, I remembered his ex and his kiddy," Ally said. An even bigger smile tugged at the corners of his mouth. "Delicious, they were. Woman was a bit frumpy and I don't usually go for blacks, but the little flower ... well, she was lovely. Just about ripe and ready for a plucking if you get me."

Hayden felt nausea and anger work through him.

Grab the gun. Grab it and shoot him and—

No don't he's goading you he's lying he's goading you he's—

"I mean I know she wasn't technically legal. And it's a shame we had to dispose of her. But some of them just ain't as cooperative as the others. Too tight, to be honest. Way too—"

Hayden snapped Ally's wrist back.

He yanked the gun away from his hand and he pressed the barrel right into his neck.

He'd expected to hear the sound of gunfire crack into his skull by now. He'd expected Gaz to pull the trigger, to end his life.

But instead, as he pressed the gun barrel further and further into Ally's neck, blocking his windpipe, making him gasp and gasp for air, he heard a thud, felt the gun slip from his head and someone dropped to the floor.

He looked to his right and he saw Gaz's body lying there, a speck of blood pooling out of his head.

Behind him, Manish was holding a loose brick from the wall and staring down at Gaz's body like he couldn't quite believe what he'd just done.

"Hayden, come on," he said. "We—we're free. We can get out of here. We can find your sister and we can get out of here."

But Hayden didn't let go. He didn't want to let go. He was pressing the barrel further into Ally's neck, watching his face go red and then purple, listening to Ally's gasps and letting Ally scratch at him and flap his hands at his face.

And he was enjoying it.

He was enjoying killing Ally.

And he was going to enjoy every moment of it.

"Hayden, we—we really need to—"

"You go," Hayden said, tensing his biceps and pressing further into Ally's neck. "I'll catch you up. I need to do this."

"I'm not going anywhere without you."

"Then wait," Hayden said. He could see saliva bubbling out of the corners of Ally's mouth, and there was almost an injustice to it. An injustice that he was being allowed to die so quick when he and the nutters at Riversford had a bunch of women chained up in that room behind. Women that had been through hell, that were going through hell, and would continue to go through hell unless he ended it, finished it, right here.

He saw Ally's eyelids flicker. His hands scratched at the concrete of the ground below. His gasps were fading away, and his face was so purple it looked like it was going to burst.

He pressed the gun in even further.

Almost there.

Almost dead.

Almost—

He didn't understand where the blast on the left side of his head came from until he was lying on his back and staring up into the darkness.

He heard some shooting, heard struggling, and then he heard someone else hit the floor beside him and he didn't understand. His ears rang, his vision blurred, clouded over, but he couldn't pass out, he couldn't let himself pass out, not now, not now ...

And then he saw Ally lean above him with a piece of loose concrete in hand. Blood was dripping from it. He smiled at Hayden with that horrid grin, said a few words to him and then laughed.

It was the laughter that struck fear through Hayden's body and mind as he drifted into blackness.

But also the thought of Sarah, the thought of his sister, both of them in line to be chained up in that awful room, both of them with a lifetime of torture ahead.

And then ...

TWENTY-NINE

Hayden was under no illusions about the situation he was in when he opened his eyes.

His head stung as a light shone at him from somewhere ahead. There was a smell—an intense smell of damp, of sick and of death, all of it rolled together as one in a horrible cocktail. He could taste blood in his mouth, clogged in his throat. His face and his head stung all over.

He remembered the room Ally had shown him. The room with the women all chained and tied up. And as he tried to move his sore wrists—finding them cuffed to a wall or somewhere behind him—Hayden's first thought was that he too was in that room. He was tied up and trapped and the men of Riversford were going to do things to him too. Terrible, awful things.

And yet it was still his sister who came to the forefront of his mind. His sister who he had to protect, no matter what.

His sister who he'd failed to protect.

He battled through the piercing light and opened his eyes. He looked around and realised he wasn't in fact in the room with the women—he was outside somewhere. Cold wind blew against his face. He was naked but for his boxer shorts, but he couldn't feel the cold on his chest or legs because his muscles must've already gone numb. His hands were tied behind his back. The light that he swore was searing was in fact nothing more than the orange glow of the setting sun in the distance.

And in front of the sun, in front of the trees that the sun was descending behind, there was a movement.

Hayden squinted and tried to focus on this movement, but it was just too out of reach for his abysmal eyes. He leaned back against the metal wall he was attached to and looked up at the reddening sky. He must've been out a while. Must've been knocked out then tied up out here then...

He spotted something in the corner of his right eye. Something he hadn't noticed before, his vision still fuzzy and blurry. Something moving.

He turned and he let out a yelp when he saw what it was.

There was a zombie tied to the wall beside him. A man with greying hair, also stripped down to his green boxer shorts. He pulled at the chains and snapped his teeth at Hayden. Bite marks lined with bruises went all down the left side of his body, which had turned a nasty shade of purple. His eyes were distant, glassy.

Hayden wondered why the Riversford group would tie a zombie up when he saw another one lurch around the side of the greying man and yank at the chains.

And then another.

And another.

Hayden held his breath. His heart picked up. He looked ahead, over at the trees again, where he'd seen the rustling of movement when he'd first opened his eyes.

He knew what was coming his way.

He knew what the movement was.

The dead.

"Shit. They—they're coming back."

The voice made Hayden swing to his left. He saw four men all tied and cuffed up to the green metal wall like him, all stripped down to their underwear, fear on their faces. One of the men was Manish. Goose pimples covered his body, and his lips looked so cold that they'd turned blue. Defrosting ice trickled down from the roof above and tapped on his shoulder, making him wince every time.

"How ... how long have we—"

"This is *frigging* it," a fat man with mid-length black hair said. "This is it. We're screwed. I don't want to die but we're screwed."

Hayden looked back at the crowd of zombies drifting their way, ever closer. Their gasps echoed against the branches of the trees. The stench of rotting flesh combined with the urinal fear of the tied up men.

Their little silhouettes got bigger, bigger.

"We have to try something," Hayden said, tugging at the cuffs around his wrists. But he realised right away just how locked in he was. The gasping zombies to his right reminded him that an uncountable number of men had tried to escape these cuffs beforehand—and an uncountable number had failed.

He tugged at the chains regardless, pulled them against the metal latches on the wall. He'd been so preoccupied with his hands that he only then realised that his feet were bound tightly at the ankles with rope. So even if he did somehow manage to get himself off this wall, he'd still be forced to hop away from a crowd of zombies that were approaching ever faster.

"Please don't let me die," a skinny blond guy who must've been in his late teens said a few down from the bald guy and Manish. "P-please don't let me die."

Hayden looked back at the metal latches they were attached to. The wall of the building was built out of corrugated steel, which wasn't ideal because it only added to its strength. But they had to try something. They had to try something or they'd die.

"We—we need to pull," Hayden said. "All of us at once. We need to pull together—"

"The hell do you think I've been tryin' for the last half an hour?" the chubby man spat.

"Please, please let me live," the blond guy whimpered.

Manish stayed still.

Hayden glanced at the approaching zombies. At least a dozen of them. And at the speed they were approaching they'd be on them in a matter of minutes—if not sooner. "All of us. At once. We need to work together if we're going to get out. So we count down from three and we pull on the wall as hard as we can. You hear me?"

"And how confident are you this is gonna work?"

Hayden wanted to tell the chubby guy that he didn't have a clue whether this was going to work or not, but also that they hardly had any better options. Instead, he said: "We have to try. We won't know if we don't try. We don't have much time."

"Please," the blond guy said. His grey boxers were drenched with piss. "I—I just want my mum. I just want my mum."

Hayden took a deep breath of the cold, stinky air. He looked ahead at the crowd of zombies. "On my count, we all pull. Ready?"

Chubby guy grunted.

Blond guy whimpered.

Manish stared on.

"Okay. On my count, we pull. Pull even if it feels like our wrists are gonna come off. We pull and we hope. Three. Two. One ... Pull!"

Hayden pulled as hard as he could and he did feel like his wrists were going to come off.

But he didn't hear a sound from the metal wall. No sign of it creaking, of morphing, or the latches snapping.

He kept on pulling. Stuck his teeth into his lips and pulled with all his strength, all his might. He closed his eyes. Closed his eyes and took his focus off the zombies ahead of him, the tied up zombies beside him, the pains in his chapped wrists and the cold in his body and the tenderness of his beaten head.

He thought of Clarice.

Imagined her in that room, chained up, beaten and bruised.

I won't let that happen to you Sis I won't let that—

He heard a snap.

His heart jumped. He opened his eyes. There was a definite sound of metal creaking, snapping.

He turned to look at the guys to see if any of them had come loose, but they were all looking at him with wide eyes.

Fearful eyes.

And then he understood.

His stomach sank, and he understood.

He held his breath. Turned to his right.

The zombie nearest him had snapped free of the chains around its bitten down wrists. The skin and flesh had been stripped away, and nothing but cracked, frail bone remained.

It hands were still in the chains, but the zombie was on its feet.

Hobbling in Hayden's direction.

THIRTY

"Fuck. Fuck. We're screwed. We're fucking screwed."

Hayden watched the zombie that had pulled itself free of the metal wall wander in his direction. He kept still—or at least, he tried to, his heart racing and his arms and legs quivering. His breath clouded up in front of him in the icy air. As he listened to the chubby guy curse and shake, he couldn't argue with him.

They were all screwed.

And he was first in line.

The zombie staggered towards Hayden. Blood dripped out from the stumpy flesh dangling out of its torn wrists, which broken bone pierced through. It looked towards Hayden with those grey, vacant eyes, and although it wasn't looking directly at him, Hayden could feel it examining his every inch—looking at the group of men chained to the wall and figuring out which one made for the best meal.

"All cause of your fucking rattling," the bald man said. There was a shaky fear to his voice now that cut through the anger. "All of your fucking rattling. Shit. Shit."

But Hayden just kept still. He kept his eyes on the zombie as it approached. Kept his eyes on it closely, but held his ground, stayed as still as he could.

It was all he could do.

Chubby guy continued to curse and twitch.

Blond guy whimpered.

At the edge of the trees just ahead, the larger group of zombies crawled ever nearer. Soon, they'd all be upon them—upon Manish, upon Hayden, upon everyone. But Hayden couldn't let that happen. He couldn't let that happen because he had a sister to look out for, a sister to protect.

And he owed it to Sarah to help her out, too. Because whatever she was going through, he knew one thing for certain about Riversford: it was no place for women.

Shit; it was no place for anyone.

"So what now?" the bald guy muttered. "What the fuck now?"

But Hayden couldn't reply. He couldn't reply because he didn't know what to say. What now? Zombies were coming for them from ahead, one of them from their right.

And he was first in line to be feasted on.

He held his breath as the putrid zombie edged closer. As it walked, its distant gaze drifted from Hayden to the other men and then back at Hayden again, like it couldn't believe its luck. Just past it, the zombies chained up to the wall pulled at their chains, and no doubt if they kept on pulling they'd be free too, and then it would be over, definitely over.

"I'm—I'm scared," the blond guy said. "I don't want to die. Please don't—don't let me die. Please."

Manish stayed quiet. So too did Hayden.

Hayden watched as the zombie edged around two feet from him. He felt his heart race. He wanted to close his eyes and turn away from his inevitable fate, but he couldn't. He couldn't divert his attention from the inevitable. It was like how you stared at a traffic accident as you drove past. There was something morbidly fascinating about death. A reminder of your own mortality standing right in front of you.

Widening its jaws.

Blood-laced saliva drooling from its chin.

He tensed all his muscles and readied himself for the impact of the teeth, for the piercing of his flesh, when he thought of his sister. Thought of Clarice. He prayed she was okay. He couldn't die. If he died, she'd have nobody to help her. And sure—Hayden had fast learned she was tough, she didn't need saving. But she still needed her brother. And he needed her.

It always had been that way.

As the snarling mouth of the zombie prepared to bite into Hayden's neck, Hayden did the only thing he could think of.

He pulled hard against the chains that his wrists were tied to.

Pulled until he heard a creaking; until his own hands felt like they were going to crack away from the cuffs.

And then he opened his own mouth as the zombie readied to bite.

He wrapped his mouth around the zombie's throat and he bit.

Hard.

The first thing he noticed was the taste. He'd heard somewhere that human flesh tasted like chicken, and that it was the body's preferred meat source simply through a case of absolute recognition.

Maybe so. But not in the case of rotting meat.

He sunk his teeth further into the zombie's neck and did all he could to keep the vomit from rising up his throat. The taste was ghastly—sour, bitter, and not aided by the smell it gave off too. He could hear the zombie gasping and groaning as cold blood dribbled down Hayden's lips, and he could hear the muffled cursing of the chubby guy and the others to his left.

But still, he kept on biting.

Kept on pulling back.

Tearing the rotting flesh from the zombie's sinewy neck.

He wondered for a split second whether he'd signed his own death warrant. In the books and the movies, sometimes all it took to turn was eating zombie flesh.

But this wasn't a book, and it wasn't a movie.

That gave him the slightest bit of hope.

While biting at the zombie's neck and trying not to pass out through sickness, he pulled and pulled at the chains, pulled because it was all he could do. His wrists were numb, his hands felt like they were going to snap away.

But he kept on pulling. For Clarice. For Sarah. For himself.

The zombie dragged itself away from Hayden and Hayden kept holding on with his teeth, being careful not to swallow any of the flesh he'd clamped down on. Muscle stretched from his neck like an elastic band, and Hayden's eye's filled with the colours of an oncoming blackout, but he kept breathing steadily, keeping his cool, pulling at the chains around his wrists.

The zombie came free of Hayden's teeth and staggered back, like it was shocked at what Hayden had done. He'd bitten a chunk out of the front of its neck; a chunk that he spat out onto the ground beside him, as well as burning stomach acid and sickly phlegm.

"Fuck, man," the chubby guy said. "You ... you ..."

But Hayden didn't hear what the chubby guy said next.

Something cracked behind him.

The feeling trickled back into his wrists.

He was free.

He sat in disbelief for a few seconds as the crowd of a dozen zombies got closer.

"You—you did it," the nervous blond guy said, eyes wide and tearful. "You ... help us. Get us out!"

Hayden looked ahead. Zombies were only ten metres or so away, and the zombie he'd bitten was right in front of them. He used his aching hands to help himself onto his feet. His ankles were still tied, but he didn't have time for them right now. Just had to hop over to Manish and the chubby guy and the nervous guy and help them, get them free, get them ...

The next thing he saw happened in a blur.

The black-haired female zombie stepping around the opposite side of the wall from out of nowhere.

Powering towards the nervous guy, who stared and screamed and shouted at Hayden as the rest of the zombies got closer.

Jumping on him.

Sinking its cracked, sharpened teeth into the top of his skull, sending blood trickling through his blond hair.

As blond guy screamed at the top of his terrified voice, screamed and begged for his mum and his dad and his everything, Hayden heard another crack to his right.

Another zombie free of the chains.

Another one to add to the dozen inching towards them.

Another marking on his death certificate.

THIRTY-ONE

If Hayden McCall knew what he was going to witness in a matter of minutes, he might've stayed on the ground and allowed the zombies to surround him.

But no man boasts the power of foresight.

"Quick, man!" the chubby guy shouted, as he shook on his chains. He stared at the nervous blond guy, who was still screaming as the zombie crunched down on the top of his head, then on his face, then on his neck, a horrible, painful way to die. "Get us the hell out of these chains! Quick!"

Hayden took in a deep breath, spat away some of the rotting taste in his mouth. A taste he figured he'd never forget or get over, not truly.

And then he looked ahead. Looked at the zombie he'd bitten standing above him, preparing to close in for another bite.

You have to get up. Get away from here. Find Sarah and Clarice and get the hell away.

He pulled himself up and lunged into the zombie's chest, his ankles still tied together. He nearly lost his balance, but the zombie tumbled away, its head cracking against the frozen, solid ground.

Behind it, he saw the dozen zombies just a matter of metres away.

A few more seconds and they'd be on him.

He turned around and hopped towards Manish.

"Hey!" the chubby guy said, bloodshot anger in his eyes. "Don't fuckin' ignore me—"

"Come on," Hayden said, pulling at the chains that were tied around Manish's wrists. It was harder than he thought. He must've pulled really damned hard to get himself free. And maybe that made him lucky.

Manish was still quiet. But he looked at Hayden right in his eyes now as the throaty cries of the zombies closed in from all directions. There were tears in his eyes, but there was a shaky smile on his face, too. "You ... you go," he said. "Go save your sister. There's not much time. Go."

"The fuck?" the chubby guy cut in. "Don't fuckin' go *anywhere*! Get me out of these damned chains."

But Hayden kept on looking into Manish's eyes and as much as he wanted to argue with him, as much as he wanted to get him from this wall and from these chains and away from here, he knew there was very little hope.

He saw a complete, resigned sincerity on Manish's face. An acceptance of what was, and of what was to be.

The ultimate sacrifice.

Hayden glanced to his left. The second zombie that had dragged itself away from the wall was fast approaching the chubby guy. Behind them, the crowd of zombies was just five metres away. So close that Hayden could feel their cold, decaying bodies surrounding him.

"There has to be a way," he said to Manish. "There has to be—"

"There is no other way," Manish said, flat smile creeping up his face again. "You—you saved me once. You gave me a chance when you could've just walked away and looked out for yourself. I'll remember that. God will remember that. Now go."

"Don't fucking go!" the chubby guy screamed, shaking and rattling at his cuffs. "Don't fucking go!"

But Hayden could only see Clarice and Sarah in his mind's eyes.

He could only hear Manish's words resounding through his mind.

"I'm sorry," Hayden said, a lump welling up in his throat. "I'm so sorry."

And then he reached down with his shaking hands, struggled to yank the ties free from his ankles, and he ran.

Ran away from the shaking and the shouting and the screaming of the chubby guy.

Ran past the oncoming crowd of zombies, pushed past them as they approached the side of the building he'd been tied to.

He wanted to look back. Wanted to look back and see that Manish was okay, that he'd made it. A small part inside him, probably inspired by video games and films with their Hollywood resolutions, pictured the chains snapping free and Manish running over and joining him at the last possible moment, the pair of them sprinting away from this hellhole and saving Clarice and Sarah from Callum and his minions.

But two things quashed that thought.

First was the squeal, so loud and high pitched that it sounded like a pig being slaughtered.

Manish.

But he didn't have the time to think about Manish's scream. He didn't have the time to think about anything when he looked ahead beyond the steel gate at the side of the building he'd been attached to.

Callum was standing in the middle of the parking area with his hands behind his back.

Beside him, two men dressed in green work slacks pointed rifles in Hayden's direction.

But it was the thing in front of them all that made Hayden's blood turn cold.

Clarice was on her knees with a gag around her mouth.

Tears rolled down her bruised cheeks.

She was stripped down to her bra and panties.

And beside her, Sarah. Same predicament, same condition.

And behind them, Ally stood, holding a long, sharp, discoloured knife.

"Don't move another muscle," Callum said.

But Hayden couldn't hear his words, not at a deep level. All he could see was his sister and his friend—his sister and his friend in that awful condition, and all he could feel was hate for these twats, these evil twats.

Blood trickled down from Sarah's swollen nose and landed on the dusty concrete.

Clarice shivered.

"You did well," Callum said, that flat smile on his face. "Getting yourself out of those chains. Lucky man. Must have some kind of god on your side. Until now, anyway. Ally."

Ally, who had a bruise around his chunky neck where Hayden had tried to strangle him, stepped up to Clarice and put the knife on Clarice's soft, tender neck.

Hayden's insides turned to stone.

He stepped forward. Stepped forward even though the two men with rifles lifted them higher, aimed at Hayden as he stood there in nothing but his boxer shorts.

Callum smiled. "I'm sorry. I really am. But you shouldn't have killed one of my men. And you definitely shouldn't have damaged the hangar wall. That's just negligence."

Ally lifted Clarice's neck. Hayden saw the fear in her tired, bruised eyes. Fear he'd seen when they were kids. He just wanted to go over there and hold her. Wrap his arms around her. Tell her everything was going to be okay.

"I don't like having to do what we're going to do," Callum said. "Seems such a waste. But you're problematic. And your sister is a part of what makes you so problematic. So you leave me with no choice." He nodded at Ally. "Go on."

He can't do it no he can't do it he won't he can't he—

Ally pulled Clarice's neck back and the next thing he saw was blood pooling out of his sister's neck and down her naked body and he heard her choking, heard her choking and struggling as Ally kept on slicing, kept on hacking away, kept on cutting.

He wanted to run at them and shout at them and scream at them but he was frozen. Frozen inside and out.

Ally kept on cutting.

Sarah looked on in total shock.

The two men with guns kept on aiming at Hayden, and Callum looked on at Clarice with a sad look on his face.

But Ally kept on cutting and cutting at Clarice's neck until it was only attached by a string of flesh.

And then he cut that piece of flesh away and he lifted her head up as blood trickled towards the ground. Her decapitated body toppled over.

He lifted Clarice's paling, wax-like head by the hair.

Smiled at Hayden, his hands and his white shirt covered in blood.

And all Hayden could do was stand there, frozen, numb, completely lost, as the first of the bullets whizzed towards him.

THIRTY-TWO

Hayden stared into the glistening blue eyes of his decapitated sister and felt the bullets whoosh over his shoulders.

"Dammit," Callum shouted. "Back up. Take her inside."

Hayden didn't understand what was happening until he heard the gasps and the groans over his shoulder. And even then he wasn't sure he cared. He was numb. Frozen. He couldn't feel anything. Not even sadness. Just nothing. A void. Like this was all some kind of horrible dream that couldn't be happening, no it couldn't be, it wasn't true because Clarice was his little sister, his little baby sister, his little baby sister who he'd sworn to look out for, sworn to protect.

His little baby sister's paling body lay headless on the concrete, the tip of her spinal cord poking out of her sliced flesh.

And her head looked back at him. Her eyes looked at him and cried for help, begged for him to help her.

But he couldn't.

And that's when he felt the anger building up inside.

He moved automatically. Moved without thought or feeling other than pure unfiltered rage. He sprinted past his sister's body, sprinted with his bare feet across the rocky ground and towards Callum and Ally and the other two men as they ran in the opposite direction, ran towards the CityFast hangar.

"Come back here!" he shouted, and his voice sounded crackly and broken. "Come the fuck back here!"

But they kept on running. One of the gunmen dragged Sarah along, dragged her up the concrete steps in front of the hangar and pulled her inside. They turned round and fired a few bullets at Hayden, but they just missed him, Hayden kept running and running and running.

He could feel the zombies approaching from behind but he didn't care. All he cared about right now was punishing Ally. Punishing Ally and Cameron and fuck—punishing all of them for what they'd done.

What they'd taken away from him.

Callum took a look back at Hayden and he mouthed something that looked like "sorry."

And then he slammed the metal door shut and he was gone, all of them were gone.

Hayden slammed face first into it. He smacked at the metal. Pulled and pushed and kicked and screamed.

"You fuckers!" he shouted, banging on the door. "You killed her you fuckers! You ... my sister. You killed her. You killed my sister."

And then Hayden pressed his head against the metal door and felt the tears rolling down his cheeks.

Clarice is dead.

They killed Clarice.

Clarice is gone.

You are alone, all alone.

He let out a shriek from deep within and dropped to his knees, his forehead still pressed up to the door. He hit the door half-heartedly as the zombies carried on their pursuit. "You killed her," he mumbled, as flashes of his little sister's first day at big school came to mind. Finding her crying by the lockers because she'd got lost, and Hayden taking her hand and showing her around and feeling good about it.

And Clarice looking back at him and smiling. Smiling with such sincerity. Such gratitude.

Gratitude that had never gone away.

"You killed her ..." he whimpered.

He heard the zombies, heard their footsteps scraping across the ground. And he heard flesh. Tearing flesh.

He spun around.

Saw one of the zombies crouched over Clarice's headless body and sinking its teeth into her belly.

"No!" he shouted. And he ran down the steps, nearly tumbled. Ran towards the zombie as it stuck its hammy fingers into her insides, pulled them out and feasted on them, Hayden's little sister's insides ...

And then he fell flat onto his face and he cried again. He shut his eyes. He couldn't look at his sister in that way. He couldn't see her in her current condition, dignity stripped from her like the flesh from her—

NO!

He sobbed on the cold ground and waited for the zombies to surround him. Waited for them to gather around and take him too. Because there was no point anymore. No point to surviving in a world where he didn't have a sister, didn't have Clarice to look out for.

I'm scared I'm scared I'm scared—

But most of all, he didn't have someone to look out for him.

He didn't have a thing to live for.

His life had lost its purpose.

He heard the footsteps and the gasps getting closer and he begged for it to happen, begged for it to be quick and over in no time.

He tensed his body and begged.

And then he thought of Sarah.

Thought of Callum and Ally. Thought of all those women tied up, beaten and bruised in that horrid chamber.

He thought of the pain they'd been through, and the pain they'd go through if he just rolled over and let them go through it.

He thought of what Clarice would say: *don't let them win. Giving up is letting them win.*

And although there was absolutely nothing he could do about it—about Sarah and Ally and Callum and those women—he knew one thing: he couldn't just die. He couldn't just give in. Not here. Not in front of Sarah.

So he stood up. Faced the two dozen zombies staggering his way. He looked past his sister's mutilated corpse and over at the gates at the front of the Riversford Industrial Estate.

He turned back. Saw a slight movement in one of the windows. And then he looked up on the roof. Shooters would be up there soon. Up there to clear the zombies from safe ground, up there to clear him.

He spat a nasty, rot tasting lump out of his mouth, and then he turned ahead.

Looked into the dead eyes of his sister's head, which had been turned in his direction by the feet of the eager zombies.

He looked at those glistening blue eyes for one final time. "I'm so sorry, Sis. I'm so sorry. So sorry."

And then he brushed his greasy, blood-soaked hair back and he ran towards the gate, away from the zombies, away from Riversford Industrial Estate.

When he looked back, Clarice's eyes weren't staring back at him.

She was gone.

THIRTY-THREE

Hayden walked alone down the centre of the Warrington road.

Cold wracked through his naked body, sent shivers right through to his core. His lips felt like they were freezing, turning icy, as the night rapidly approached. His head stung—stung with the physical pains of the beatings he'd taken, but mostly with the emotional turmoil that ran riot through his skull.

The memories of Ally pulling his sister's head back.

Slicing the knife across her neck.

Spraying her blood out all over the concrete outside the Riversford Industrial Estate and leaving her to drown in her own fluids.

And Hayden not being able to do a thing about it.

He heard a noise somewhere behind him. The sound of peppering gunfire. The Riversford group cleaning up the zombies, no doubt. Cleaning up what they didn't want, just like they always would. Because that's the kind of world they lived in now—a world where the people willing to take what they wanted and exploit it for their own selfish needs succeeded.

A world where Hayden didn't want to live.

But a world that had taken his sister away from him.

And for that reason, a world that had to pay.

He carried on walking down the middle of the cracked concrete, past the abandoned cars and boarded up buildings, not really paying any attention to his surroundings or where he was going. Only that he needed time. Time to think. Time to prepare.

Time to prepare for *something*.

He tasted blood on his lips and he remembered the sacrifice Manish had made to allow Hayden to power on and save his sister, save Sarah. He remembered the blood-curdling sound of Manish's scream—and what had he died for? For Clarice to have her head sliced from her body right in front of Hayden. For Sarah, all battered and bruised, to be taken back inside the *CityFast* hangar to an inevitable fate of pain and suffering.

All because a group of power-crazy men had a twisted utopian vision.

All because they thought, somewhere in their messed up minds, that they were saving the world.

There was no saving the world. Hayden understood that now. There was only saving yourself. Saving those you cared about. There was no system, no greater force swooping in to save anyone, no trust.

It was survival of the fittest. A Darwinian paradise; a snapshot of natural selection.

Adapt or become one of the mindless masses. Become one of the zombies, one of the primary citizens of the new world.

Hayden stopped when he reached a crossroads. He stared down the road, peppered with broken glass and specks of blood. The wind was strong, and it whooshed through the smashed windows of the empty shops. Up ahead, Hayden could see a range of snow-swept mountains, and a part of him just wanted to go up there to the top and freeze to death.

But another part inside him wanted to go back to Riversford and die trying to save Sarah.

He just didn't know how.

He lowered his head and kept on walking when he heard the footsteps to his left.

He stopped. Looked up. No sign of life by the abandoned shops. No sign of death either. He was cold. His mind was playing with him. That's all this was—the cold was getting to him and he was in shock.

He started walking when he heard the noise again.

This time, he realised it wasn't as near as he first thought. It was far away, somewhere in the distance, like a voice echoing from afar, or the sound of a television turned down really quietly.

But there was something. A definite movement. Footsteps.

Everything inside Hayden told him to turn around. Walk away. Head back to Riversford and find a way inside; find a way to die trying to save Sarah, save the other women tied up in that outhouse.

But instead, he found himself walking towards the noise. Following it like a child chasing the pot of gold at the foot of the rainbow.

Because he had an idea. Out of nowhere, he had an idea.

He moved the numb soles of his feet against the icy road and he stopped when he saw exactly what the source of the noise was.

In the distance, up one of the hills, he could see a large mass of zombies. A mass much like the ones that had attacked the bunker, and like the ones that had swarmed out of the trees and forced him, Clarice and Newbie off the road. Probably the same group following Hayden all this way in search of their meal.

His heart thumped. The fragments of an idea formed in his weak, stunned mind. He'd hardly had a chance to process his sister's death—and all the other losses he'd suffered—but right now he had something. Something to try. Something to attempt.

He saw that the group of zombies was wandering mostly in the opposite direction, and he figured the smaller group that had

Felt another drip of bitter snot dribble d

I won't let you die without a fight, Sis. I ι
what they've done. I won't let Sarah die the sa

He stared at the mass of hundreds c
of Warrington.

He opened his mouth.

And at the top of his voice, he shoutε

THIRTY-FOUR

"I ... I dunno whether I can do this anymore. I dunno whether I can do this."

Callum Hessenthaler stared out at the piles of undead stretched across the grounds of Riversford Industrial Estate. As the sun made its final descent, he figured his men had done a good job of cleaning up the mess. Now was the iffy case of burning the bodies, disposing of them. Usual procedure whenever there was a breach like this—which admittedly was more common than Callum would've liked.

But his main problem right now was the whiney fool, Jared, who was acting like a blubbering mess ever since Ally had sliced the girl's head off.

Callum turned around and looked at his men. Three of them were gathered around his desk, lit up in an orange glow by the setting sun. Jared, a well-built man with a black beard that hid his face in the way that so many men chose to do nowadays, was rubbing his hands against the blood-soaked arms of his green CityFast jumpsuit. Ally and Martin were here, too—two of his more obedient foot soldiers of the twenty-three people that made up his team. Ally in particular.

"You'll be fine," Callum said, grabbing a half-empty bottle of Evian from his desk and sipping it back, savouring the cold as it kissed his lips. "You've done well so far. Everyone gets stressed from time to time. That's forgivable in the circumstances."

But Jared's lips were quivering. His tired eyes were filling up with the little red worms of bloodshot. He looked like a man with something to say.

They always looked like this when they had something to say.

Callum sat at his desk and leaned back in the beautifully comfortable ergonomic chair. He sipped some more of the water. He liked to limit himself to a solitary sip per hour to stave any potential drought. But today had been a tough day. An especially tough day. So he deserved to treat himself. "Is this going to be a problem, Jared?"

Jared opened his mouth then closed it again as if thinking twice about what he was going to say. And then he opened his mouth, glanced up at Ally and said, "The girl. She was just an innocent girl. There was no need to ... what you did. There was no need."

Callum glanced at Ally. He wanted to see Ally's reaction. There was something fascinating about Ally. He was like a rescued pit bull with a previous history of mauling. When Callum first came into possession of this Riversford Industrial Estate—when he first encountered the idea of farming women for sexual entertainment and the breeding of a new generation—he always imagined he'd have to train somebody to do the dirty work, to do the things that went beyond the limits and the boundaries of a normal human being. But Ally came pre-trained, packaged and ready to bite.

That was a major bonus. It had got the Riversford group a long way in a short time.

When he looked at Ally, he didn't see a glimmer of remorse on his, admittedly handsome, face. Just a roll of the eyes and the flicker of a smile. "She was a troublemaker. She was the only thing her bastard brother cared about. So now she's gone he's as good as dead. Win-win."

"But she was an innocent girl," Jared said, and he spoke louder this time. Colour seeped into his face. He looked like he was holding his breath underwater, his lungs ready to burst with a thousand repressed thoughts and feelings.

Callum stood up. Stepped over the speck of blood on the freshly polished tiles. Walked over to Jared.

He stood right in front of him. Stared up at him. "Lift your chin and look into my eyes."

"I'm sick of—of your games. I just want my wife back. I just want my wife and—"

Callum lifted Jared's chin so that he was staring right into his eyes. He glared into them. Saw a glimmer of fear, but mostly anger. Anger Callum knew was directed at him.

Anger he had to control.

Callum reached slowly into his back pocket for his knife, his hands getting shaky and sweaty. "I'd think very carefully about your next words. Remember your place here. You turned up here looking for security and a safe haven. You asked for our help—"

"Not like this," Jared said, shaking his head. "Not like this."

Callum wrapped his fingers around the knife. He could feel the urge getting stronger. It was an urge he'd never really felt before the world went to pot—aside from the occasional frustration at a parking attendant when they charged him extra for a pay and display ticket, or at a client who spent their day shouting on the phone to him like the errors of his company were solely his responsibility.

But there was something liberating about the urge to kill in the new world. A way to cleanse one's self of all frustrations, start afresh and clear the mind, much like a horny teenager masturbates to work off the day's frustration.

He could see Ally's smile growing and he felt the hunger, felt the bloodlust.

He moved the knife from behind his back.

And then he stopped.

"I think you're right," Callum said.

He let go of Jared's chin. Put the knife in his pocket and stepped back.

Jared's eyes narrowed. He looked at Callum with confusion. "I ... what ..."

"Maybe we have been doing things wrong around here. Maybe our system does lack a little ... equality. Boys, put him on the floor."

Ally and Martin looked equally surprised but still they complied, grabbing Jared by his arms and pushing him down to the floor.

Callum felt himself getting hard. He snapped his belt away and pulled his trousers down to his ankles. His penis bulged out, and he felt the frenzy spreading to it, spreading to it and begging him to assert his dominance, his control, in another way. "Pull down his trousers."

Ally and Martin still looked confused, bewildered, but like angry dogs they tore Jared's trousers and revealed his bare ass as Jared screamed and shouted and punched the floor.

Callum stepped around him. He crouched down, put his hands on Jared's plump ass cheeks while Ally let out a little excited laugh and pulled down his trousers too, and then Martin did the same like this was all some kind of filthy joke between a bunch of teenagers.

Callum leaned down and pressed himself towards Jared's asshole. He breathed in his ear. "You wanted equality? How's this for equality?"

And then Jared screamed even louder when Callum pressed himself inside him.

He screamed even louder when Ally joined in and then Martin joined in, all of them laughing, frenzied, like cats playing with an injured mouse.

But the loudest scream came when Callum pulled the blade out and stuffed it up Jared's asshole.

They were so caught in the bloodlust, so caught in the frenzy that they didn't see the mass of zombies staggering towards the entrance gates of the Riversford Industrial Estate.

They didn't see Hayden leading them.

THIRTY-FIVE

When Hayden heard the panicked shouts, he knew he was in business.

He looked over his shoulder and down the road towards the front entrance of the Riversford Industrial Estates. The zombies that he'd caught up with, that he'd led down here, were wandering towards the gates. There were hundreds of them —and perhaps the gates would keep them from entering.

But whether they did or not was irrelevant.

What was relevant was that Hayden had his distraction.

He ran over to a garbage container and climbed onto its icy surface. The night was drawing in, but it didn't matter to Hayden, not anymore. He was beyond cold. He knew he'd likely die of hypothermia if he didn't wrap up soon.

But first, he had to get inside Riversford. He had to get inside the CityFast HQ. He had to find a key in Callum's office, and he had to save Sarah and the other women tied up in that chamber.

There was something else he needed to do, too.

Something niggling away at him. Something he couldn't avoid, couldn't deny, no matter what.

He had to kill Callum and Ally.

He had to make them pay for what they'd done to Clarice.

He peeked over the top of the chain-linked fence at the tall metallic CityFast structure. There were a few people out on the roof, all firing at the zombies that were gathered at the main gate. There was a couple of other guards running around the grounds outside—running over the remains of the zombies they'd butchered earlier.

Running over Clarice's remains ...

Hayden held his breath and grabbed the cold metal at the top of the fence. He knew there was barbed wire laced just above his hands, but that too was a risk he was willing to take, willing to accept.

Right then, as he dragged himself over the fence and felt the blades nicking his naked arms and chest, he was willing to die if it meant getting the vengeance that Clarice deserved.

He didn't care what kind of person it made him, how many ethical or moral bullshit codes it breached.

He had to be savage.

He felt rain peppering down from the darkened skies as he crept across the stony gravel. He could hear voices nearby, as the lights from torches flickered around the ground, the speckles of bullets illuminated the dying day like fireworks, and the zombies sang and pressed and pushed up to the fences.

He kept himself low and approached some metal scaffolding at the side of the CityFast structure as the icy rain came down heavier—actually somewhat refreshing. He looked up at the scaffolding. He could see a window five storeys up, which had to be Callum's place. He'd made a note of how many floors he climbed when he was taken up there earlier. He had a feeling he'd need that information at some stage.

He put his hands on the icy, wobbly metal frames of the scaffolding and he dragged himself up.

He wasn't best pleased about heights, but he couldn't let any fears in, not now.

He climbed up a few of the poles and the wind and rain got heavier. Water splashed in his eyes. The poles of scaffolding wobbled and creaked on their hinges. And as he ascended, he could constantly hear the firing of rifles at the zombies, the shouting of troops, the—

A piece of scaffolding snapped away.

He felt himself descending.

Grabbed around for something, anything, and ...

His fingers wrapped around the edge of a rough slab of wood, multiple splinters piercing the tips of his fingers.

But he couldn't shout. He couldn't cry out. He just had to go with it. Go with it and climb.

He steadied his breathing, blinked the rainwater out of his eyes and climbed higher. The window was just metres away now. He could get in there. Get in there and find the keys to the chamber outside where the women were being kept. And sure, getting to that chamber while a ground battle was going on was a challenge in itself. But he had to take things one step at a time. He couldn't think too far ahead. Think too far ahead, and he'd slip, slip down below to the icy ground ...

He was just a few inches away from the window when he saw movement in there.

He slowed his movement. Climbed more carefully. He didn't want to risk being seen, not now.

And then he heard a voice. Muffled, unclear. "Swear I heard summat," or something like that.

The window clicked open.

A bay window, which a man in a green hat stepped out of.

Walked to the edge.

Looked down.

Hayden didn't recognise this man as he stared him in his green eyes, long blade in his right hand. But he knew that by being here, this man was involved in the death of his sister, one way or another.

He didn't know the man's past. He didn't know if the man had been a good dad who'd been led astray by Callum, he didn't know if this man had family chained up in that chamber and was only abiding by Callum's sick laws to get by. He didn't know a thing.

But that didn't stop him grabbing the man's ankle.

Yanking him from the balcony.

Sending him screaming, tumbling down to the ground below.

He didn't know a thing about the man. But seconds later, he knew exactly what the man sounded like when his head split open and cracked on impact.

Hayden kept still for a few seconds. He swore he'd heard the man speaking to someone behind the bay window, which was rattling in the wind. He didn't want to risk being ambushed. So he kept as cool as he could. Kept on looking, listening, waiting.

Nothing.

He dragged himself slowly to the top of the scaffolding and peeked in through the bay window.

He could see the large glass window at the opposite side of the room he'd stood in when Callum Hessenthaler had revealed his fate. He could see the desk that Callum had sat writing at when he'd first walked in.

The desk that the keys had to be in. They had to be.

He climbed into the window and was met with a refreshing sense of warmth as he walked through into the room. He could hear the water and sweat dripping onto the floor from his body. But he couldn't stick around—he had to act fast. Had to get to the desk.

He rushed across the room, heart pounding, and he stopped when he saw what was on the tiles in front of the desk.

There was a man he didn't recognise. He had dark hair and a bushy beard. His green trousers were around his ankles.

A knife was wedged into his anus, and his throat was cut.

"Faggot" had been sliced into his pale head.

But it was his eyes that scared Hayden the most. The eyes that still looked so alive. And yet so terrified.

He took a deep breath and tried not to puke as he walked around the side of Callum's desk, walked past the man's blood, and crouched down to look in the drawers.

The first drawer was empty but for a photograph. Callum Hessenthaler and a young girl standing in front of the Eiffel Tower, smiles on their faces. It was like seeing one of your favourite TV actors in a new show, struggling to adapt to the difference in role.

Hayden checked the second drawer—still no key, but a leather-bound notepad. The one Callum had been scribbling in when Hayden first walked in here.

He reached down, the gunshots still peppering outside. He unclipped the little button that covered the front.

When he saw what was inside, the nausea cranked up a decibel.

There was no writing. No writing on any of the pages. No autobiographical accounts or stories of survival.

There were just doodlings.

Doodlings of women with their legs tied to walls behind them by their ankles, blood dribbling from their genitals.

Pictures of piles and piles of men slicing the necks of women with identical knives while engaging in intercourse with them.

Page after page of dead women, dead children, dead ...

It was at that moment that Hayden became suddenly aware that somebody was watching him. A feeling he couldn't deny and yet had no logical explanation—just that sense that something in the atmosphere has changed.

He looked up. Looked around the office. It seemed to have gone quieter outside. The bay window rattled in the wind.

Nothing in here.

He crouched down again and reached into the final drawer and his heart leapt.

There was a rusty key on a beaded chain. A key just like the one Ally had used to open the door to the chamber where the women were kept.

He reached in. Snatched the key out of the drawer. Stood up.

"I think you should put that back, don't you?"

Hayden heard the voice before he saw where it was coming from.

But when he saw him, he got that horrid feeling again, as the rain battered against the windows and screams rang out from the grounds below.

Callum Hessenthaler was standing by the stairs in front of Hayden.

And he was pointing a pistol at him.

THIRTY-SIX

"Put the key back in the drawer and step towards me. Slowly."

Hayden's heart pounded the second he laid eyes on Callum. His thin hair and his grey suit were completely dry, which meant he had to have been inside all along. His steady hands pointed the pistol right at Hayden's chest as he stood behind Callum's desk. The wind blew specks of rain and gusts of cold air in through the open bay window. The sounds of gunshots and shouting rang out from the battle with the zombies outside.

"Don't make this more painful for you than it has to be," Callum said. He raised the gun even higher. "Put the key back in the drawer or I swear I'll shoot you right here. And I don't want to shoot you all over my desk. It's top drawer mahogany. Nobody wants to ruin top drawer mahogany."

The way Callum spoke was so cold, and yet it didn't surprise Hayden. Not after the doodling he'd seen in Callum's "book." "See your recording of events is going well," Hayden said, as he crouched down to place the key back into the drawer.

Or at least, to find something. Anything he could use.

Callum's stone face didn't even twitch. "There are different kinds of artists in the world. Word artists, visual artists, musical artists. I tried my hand at writing. Wasn't for me. Did you like the drawings?"

Hayden tasted sick in the back of his throat as he remembered the black ink scribbling of women being torn apart by the disproportionate erect penises of knife-wielding men. "Acquired taste, I think."

Callum's smile twitched at this. He kept on pointing the gun. "Step over here, Hayden. Drop the key right there. Come from behind my desk. I don't want to have to clean this place up again."

Hayden kept hold of the key, mid-crouch. He knew what would happen if he tried to search one of the other drawers. Callum would shoot him there and then. He'd clocked on to Hayden's plan. Hayden was taking far too long.

He needed something. Anything.

"Not content with a dozen murders for the day?"

"What happened to your sister was regrettable," Callum said, and there was a look on his face like he was genuinely remorseful. "It's our role here to protect our women. But she was proving problematic. Don't you see that? And, now here you are and conveniently, here a mass of zombies are. I'm assuming your selfishness had something to do with them?"

Hayden dropped the key into the top drawer. It dropped onto the photograph of Callum and his daughter. He wanted to reach in there, grab it, but he was cornered. It was no use.

"Step out here and get on your knees in front of Jared," Callum said. Hayden assumed the poor mutilated man on the office floor had to be Jared. "I'll make it quick if you don't put up a fight."

But Hayden couldn't move. He couldn't step towards Callum. If he stepped towards Callum, he'd be signing his own death warrant. Signing his death warrant for the man who'd sanctioned the murder of his sister.

No. He couldn't give up. He had to find Sarah. Help her.

And he had to make these bastards pay for what they'd done to Clarice.

"Have you ever lost someone right in front of your own eyes?" Hayden asked. He felt his throat swelling up. The sounds of Clarice's wheezing and gurgling through her sliced windpipe scratched at the corners of his sanity, but he couldn't let those thoughts in, not now, not ever.

He saw Callum's eyes cloud over. Rain battered against the wide open window that overlooked the dark premises of the night-drenched Riversford Industrial Estate. "I have, as a matter of fact. Lost my wife in a skiing accident. Held her hand while she was in a coma for days, weeks. Felt the life slip out of her body when the doctors finally decided enough was enough.

"I was catatonic at first, of course. I was frustrated. Frustrated with the system for giving up on her. Furious with the people who'd allowed her to die. Annoyed with myself, in a way, for even allowing her to go on a skiing holiday with her friends. But now I look back ... I think putting her to rest was the right decision. Because waking up from a state like the one she was in would've been cruel. And no beauty thrives in the cruellest of worlds."

Hayden noticed the complete glassiness to Callum's eyes.

The gun was still pointed at him, but there was a stillness. Like somebody had hit the pause button on life and frozen the two men's differences in time.

A stillness that Hayden had to exploit.

He ducked his head and yanked open one of the drawers and he heard the reactionary blast from Callum's gun.

Heard the large window smash open, felt the gust of wind and rain work its way inside.

"Get the hell from behind that desk and stand up like a man," Callum said. There was panic in his voice now. Footsteps pounded against the tiles. Hayden knew he didn't have long. He knew he couldn't just dance around the desk and hope Callum would avoid him like a confused dog.

He looked at the edge of the cracked window, gunshots flickering outside.

Saw a sharp shard of glass sticking up loosely from the bottom corner. Large enough to stick through Callum's throat, large enough to finish him.

Footsteps getting closer.

He had to do something.

He held his breath and threw himself at the shard of glass, wrapped his fingers around it and felt the sharpness cut through his skin as he tried to yank it free.

And then he felt his face hit the floor.

Felt Callum grabbing the side of his body and twisting him over.

He pinned Hayden down. Crouched onto him and pinned him down. There was a manic look to his eyes. Manic. Bloodshot. The cool control of before was gone, replaced by a predator of a man.

He started to move the gun around to point at Hayden. "I said I'd make it quick, but now I'm not so sure. You ruined my damned window. Do you realise how much I liked standing and looking out of that window?"

Hayden stretched his right hand out to the drawer. Felt the metal of the handle tap against the tips of his fingers. Just had to stretch a little further. Just a little further ...

Callum brought the gun to Hayden's forehead and pressed so hard into it that it felt his skull was going to crack. "I'm going to enjoy this. I'm going to enjoy this like I would've enjoyed doing it to your sister." Hayden could feel a bulge in Callum's trousers, saw him salivating at the corners of his mouth. "I'm going to—"

The next couple of seconds were a blur.

Hayden got a grip on the metal handle of the drawer.

He pulled the heavy wood drawer out of place and smacked it into the side of Callum's head.

And then a blast crashed through his skull and he swore he'd been shot as his ears rang, like the eardrums had been ripped open, but then he realised he couldn't have been shot because he was thinking these thoughts.

Callum fell to Hayden's left.

Hayden swung himself onto him, grabbed the gun, which Callum fired aimlessly and blasted at the ceiling.

Callum wasn't letting go. He wouldn't stop holding the gun.

So Hayden wrapped his teeth around Callum's wrist until he pierced the flesh and the muscle while Callum screamed and kicked and whimpered in agony.

And then the gun came loose.

Hayden grabbed the gun as it fell from Callum's hand and pointed it at Callum. He stepped away so Callum couldn't take a swing of it. Backed off as blood dripped down Callum's head from the impact of the wooden drawer. "On your feet," Hayden said.

Callum shook his head. "I—I won't—you don't—"

Hayden pointed at Callum's right hand and fired.

Clean shot. Slammed into his fingers and took four of them off.

Callum whined in agony and stared at his fingers in shock. He was so pale, he looked like he was going to puke.

"Now get the fuck up or I'll make this as slow and as painful as possible," Hayden said.

Callum shook his head. "I ... you fuck. You don't question me. You don't—"

Hayden fired another round into Callum's forearm—the opposite to the one he'd chewed.

Callum screamed again as blood splattered out of it.

"Now get on your feet. I mean it."

Callum shook as he struggled to stand. "I ... What happened to your sister. I'm sorry. I truly am, if that's what you want to hear."

"Step back to the window."

Callum looked nervously over his shoulder. The open mouth of the massive window he'd cracked with his own shot stared back at him, waited to swallow him up. "Please," he said. "You've ... you've proven me wrong. You're a good soldier. A good fighter. We could do with—"

"Back up to the window and I'll think about letting you live."

Callum stood still. Tears dripped down his pale cheeks as blood dribbled from his gunshot wounds. His jaw shook, and he looked a fraction of the calm, cool man Hayden had first met when he'd reached this place. "My daughter. I still have a daughter out there. She's—"

"Back up to the window and I'll let you live."

Callum's eyebrows narrowed. "I ... I ..."

"Just do it."

Callum hesitated and then shuffled back a couple of steps. The wind from the open window brought in an icy gust of rain, drenching Callum as he stood helplessly at the edge.

He looked Hayden right in the eyes. "Show mercy. Please. You don't want to make the—the mistakes I've made. You don't want to live with that on your conscience."

Hayden lowered the gun. He started to turn. "I'll show mercy," he said.

And then he turned back around and fired two bullets in each of Callum's kneecaps.

"Don't slip."

But Callum did slip.

He fell backwards as the bullets smashed through his kneecaps.

He struggled and scrambled to grab the cracked edges of the windows but only sliced his hands in the process.

"Please!" he shouted, as he tumbled back. "Plea ..."

His final "please" was drowned out by a scream.

He fell out of the window.

Disappeared into the night.

Hayden waited until he heard the cracking of bones before moving.

When he did, he walked back to the drawer, grabbed the key, and walked away.

Next stop: Sarah.

THIRTY-SEVEN

Hayden stepped outside the CityFast entrance to the sound of gunshots and gasping.

He was dressed in the green uniform the rest of Callum's men wore. He'd found a spare on his way down. The hangar was so empty it was alarming, and it reminded Hayden that for all the apparent organisation of the place, a zombie attack still had the capability to upset all order.

It was like an ant's nest. The queen had been butchered, and the rest of the little ants were running round in a frenzy.

Now he just had to rescue Sarah and the other tied-up women from the centre of the nest before the boiling water that was the zombies perished them all.

He walked slowly and kept himself low as he moved across the grounds. To his left, he could hear the gates squeaking as the mass of zombies he'd led here pressed up to them. It was dark, but Hayden could see an indentation forming in the metal—a sure sign that the gate wasn't going to hold forever. Standing at the other side were at least six men, all firing at the zombies. But firing at them was doing nothing. More zombies were just taking the places of the ones who'd been executed. It was like respawned enemies in video games. No matter what you did, no matter how many you killed, they just kept on coming.

He held the gun in one hand and the key in the other. He moved as fast as he could across the rain-soaked concrete, the water covering the top of the brown Timberlands that were definitely a size too small for him. He'd never been fond of the darkness since the outbreak, but right now it felt like the darkness was his friend. The darkness was a tool he had to use to get into the chamber where the women were being kept, get them out of here and then flee—flee with all of them.

How he was going to get them free, he wasn't sure yet. But it was one decision at a time. Look too far ahead at the mountain you have to climb, you risk stepping on a landmine right in front of you.

He could taste the metallic tang of blood as he reached the middle of the yard, turned his attention to the rusty door that the chamber was through. His blood, the blood of the zombie he'd bitten the neck of, the blood from Callum's wrist. But the blood mostly made him think of his sister. Reminded him of the blood that had spurted out of her neck.

Memories he wanted to rid his mind of, memories and a reality he didn't want to face up to.

Memories he couldn't avoid.

He was within five metres of the rusty door when he saw a man dressed in green CityFast slacks step out from beside it.

He stopped, convinced the man had seen him. He was a big man—definitely bigger than Hayden, so not somebody he wanted to mess with. Blond hair and a ginger beard. His face was pale, and Hayden could see the nervousness in him as he twitched with his rifle.

Hayden saw the man's eyes look right at him. He saw them connect with his—saw a glimmer of recognition, a glimmer of understanding.

So Hayden lifted the gun and readied to fire.

But then the man looked away, looked past Hayden and wandered in the other direction like he hadn't seen Hayden at all.

Hayden couldn't understand. A part of him wanted to believe that the guard hadn't seen him. A part of him wanted to believe that he *had* seen him, but his morals had got the better of him and he was giving Hayden a chance to go in that chamber and save the innocent people chained up.

Hayden wanted one of those two options so badly.

But he couldn't be certain any of them was more than just hopeful speculation.

So he lifted the pistol and fired it just once into the side of the blond guy's head.

The noise of the gunshot alarmed Hayden. But when he looked over at the gates, he realised it was lost to the sounds of other bullets firing, to other shouts and cries.

He ran up beside the man. Looked down at him lying on the floor with a hole in the side of his head that blood was trickling out of.

"Sorry," Hayden said.

And then he took the man's rifle and ran towards the rusty metal door.

As he moved, he got a flash of the fear he'd felt when he'd pulled the trigger on the guy called Dave back at the cottage. Shit —it was only earlier today, and yet it felt like a lifetime ago. So much had happened since. So many things that had changed who he was, *what* he was.

He compared the emotions he'd felt when he killed Dave to the emotions he'd felt when he'd killed this nameless blond guy and the comparison scared him.

It scared him, but he didn't have the time to ponder that fear right now.

He reached the door. Stuffed the rusty key inside it. As he turned the key, he wondered whether he'd made a mistake, the door staying firmly shut and not budging.

But then it clicked open.

He turned the handle. Caught a whiff of urine, of sweat and faeces.

He was inside.

He looked back at the fences outside. Even more of an indentation forming, lit up by the gunfire—which was growing more sporadic. Some of the men were retreating, pulling back. Soon, the place would be overrun. He had to think. He had to act.

Now or never.

He stepped into the damp, narrow corridor and made his way through the darkness to the chamber door. He felt like he was walking forever, trapped in an awful nightmare. He felt his heart pick up as he became disoriented, losing sight and sense of his surroundings—had he come in from the left? Or the right?

Was he stuck in here?

Was there something else down this corridor he didn't know about?

And then he felt something cold and metallic hit his face and he looked down and saw the dim glow of light peeking out of the door.

He held his breath, the sour smell of suffering intensifying. From outside, he heard the loudest shouts of all, heard snapping and breaking.

And then he heard a blood-curdling shout from the room in front of him.

He went rigid. Completely still. He swore the women were all gagged when he'd last been in here. And yet that scream seemed so ... clean.

He put his hand on the handle. Lowered it. Pushed the door open.

Please Sarah please Sarah please.

The door creaked open.

It took Hayden a few seconds to comprehend what he was looking at inside.

The only thing he comprehended right away was Ally's smile as he stood behind a blonde haired woman.

A blonde haired woman whose throat had been slit.

THIRTY-EIGHT

Hayden heard the zombies break through the gates of the Riversford Industrial Estate, but his focus was elsewhere.

On the women, all chained up, blood drooling out of their sliced throats.

Five, six, seven of them, all dead, all sitting in a pool of their own piss and blood.

Ally standing there behind another of the women, blood trickling down from his knife and onto the floor of the dusty, damp chamber.

Hayden stared at him for a few seconds, and Ally stared back. There was a confusion in Ally's eyes—a confusion of Hayden being here, especially when he was supposed to be gone, supposed to be dead.

But there was a look of triumph, too. An inevitability that Hayden should be back here.

A chance to finish him off like he'd wanted to all along.

Hayden heard a mumbling to his right. He looked and he saw Sarah chained up, stripped down. For the first time in a long time, Hayden saw fear in her glazed blue eyes.

Ally turned to her. Looked at her.

And then, with his knife raised, he walked over to her.

Hayden didn't even have to think twice about lifting the rifle he'd taken from the guard he'd killed and firing at Ally.

But it jammed. The trigger wouldn't budge. His video game knowledge of weapons had failed him.

Ally rushed closer towards Sarah, his footsteps splashing in the pools of blood. The room was like an abattoir—*worse* than an abattoir.

He'd killed countless women. He'd murdered the whole screwed up reason for this place's existence. The captain wasn't going down with the sinking ship—his second-in-command was making damned sure the passengers came down with him.

He grabbed the back of Sarah's head.

Pulled her neck back.

Hayden threw himself at Ally and sent him crashing into the concrete wall behind. Adrenaline raced through his body. He clutched his arm to make sure he couldn't stab him, grabbed him by his scrawny neck and wrapped his hands around tightly.

A smack on the right side of Hayden's face. His head went dizzy, his vision went blurry, the sound of the chaos outside faded out.

Hayden tried to regain his ground and then he felt another smack against his face, and this one was enough to send him flying back to the floor and smacking his head on the cold, blood-dampened tiles.

Ally sat down on his belly and lifted the knife.

Hayden struggled to get his hands free, smacked at the side of Ally's head as the knife came crashing towards his chest, and then shifted out of the way just in time.

"You're a fighter," Ally said, as Hayden gripped tight hold of the hand he had the knife in. Sweat dripped down from Ally's smiling face. "Pity you couldn't fight for your sister when I sawed her head off, huh?"

Hayden slammed his palm into the arm that was supporting Ally, sent him slipping to the floor.

He tried to climb back onto Ally so he had the advantage but Ally elbowed him right in the stomach, knocked the wind out of him in a sickening blow.

Ally stood up. He pulled his foot back and booted Hayden right between his eyes. His head smacked against the tiles again, made him even dizzier, clouded his vision even more. He tried to get back up, but whenever he did, he felt Ally's heavy boot crack his mouth again. He tasted blood, something solid in there too—a tooth that Ally had knocked free.

Hayden tried to rise again, but he was down, he was too weak, he couldn't take another kick, couldn't take another.

"Hear that?" Ally shouted, and Hayden didn't hear it because his ears were ringing too loudly. "That's the sound of death coming our way."

He pulled back his boot and smacked his foot into Hayden's left ribs so hard that Hayden couldn't breathe.

"It's been coming our way since the start of this bullshit outbreak. I'm not deluded like Callum. Known all along that this whole new society shit was a load of crap. But hey. I got some fun out of it. Your sister could vouch for that, huh?"

Hayden's skin tingled and his body burned with rage but when he tried to lift himself, tried to shift his weakened muscles, Ally just booted him again, booted him right in the neck this time so that his breathing grew harder, swallowing impossible.

Ally crouched down over Hayden, leaned so close into his face that Hayden could see his demonic smile through the blur. "You're a fighter, and I respect that. But you're always gonna lose. You're weak. You couldn't save your sister, so like fuck are you gonna save your bitch, save yourself."

Ally lifted the knife. Pushed it right up to Hayden's throat. Hayden felt it piercing his skin, felt it working its way through the outer layers, soon to cut through the muscle and puncture his throat.

He felt the indentation in his pocket. Felt the indentation and knew it was all he had.

The rusty key on the metal beaded chain.

"You'll suffer for ... for this," Hayden said. He wrapped his weak fingers around the bead of the chain.

Ally laughed. "Heh. Don't get all biblical on me now. I'd have brought a priest along for your last rites but I'm not sure now's the place for—"

Hayden shifted his neck to the right.

He felt it pierce through the entire left side of his skin, his flesh, as Ally's weight dropped and the knife hit the floor.

And then with all he had—with the only strength he had left inside him—he lifted the metal chain and wrapped it around Ally's neck.

Tight.

Ally struggled. He struggled and pulled away at the flap of skin and muscle he'd cut from Hayden's neck. Yanked the knife away, tore right through it, sending agony searing through Hayden's body.

But Hayden was free.

Bleeding, probably fatally wounded, but free.

Hayden took his opportunity and got behind Ally. He thought of his sister, thought of the fear in her eyes, thought of the pain this man had put her through and he tightened his grip, tightened the chain, harder, harder, harder.

Ally struggled and spluttered. He punched and kicked out and hurt Hayden more and more, but Hayden wasn't budging. He was standing his ground. He was finishing the job.

"You killed her," Hayden said, rage and adrenaline coursing through his body. "You killed my sister and you ... you will say her name. Clarice. You will say her name and you will apologise."

Ally struggled and spluttered. His cheeks were turning purple. Bubbly saliva spewed out from his greyed-out lips.

"You'll say her fucking name and you will apologise!" Hayden said.

He felt warm tears rolling down his cheeks as he held Ally, squeezed tighter and tighter around his neck, so tight that the metal chain was digging into his skin and piercing through.

He held on, his knuckles white, his heart racing, the thought of his sister in his mind—his sister smiling at him, thanking him for being there for her, holding his hand and telling him what a good big brother he was.

"You'll say her name," Hayden sputtered through his tears. "You'll—you'll say her name."

He wasn't sure how much longer he held on to that chain around Ally's neck.

Ally stopped struggling.

His muscles loosened.

And when Hayden pulled the chain out of the deep crevices it had formed in Ally's neck, the last thing he heard Ally whisper was, "Clar ..."

THIRTY-NINE

The first emotion that entered Ally Harbridge's mind when he opened his tender eyes was one of relief.

His vision was blurry and fuzzy. The stench of blood was strong in the air—so strong. Even though it hurt to breathe, sent a shiver right through his body and sharp pains right through his chest, he was relieved. Because he was alive. That bastard Hayden didn't have the guts to finish him off after all.

Weak. Weak, just like his sister.

He blinked a few times and tried to focus properly on his surroundings, tried to understand where he was. There was a dim light dangling above him. The same dim light he saw every time he came in this chamber to see to his women. Yes. The chamber. He was in the chamber. Hayden had beaten him and left and ...

He tried to edge forward and felt something sharp dig right into his chest. He reached over to see what it was but his arms wouldn't move and trying to move them just crippled his shoulder.

Same thing happened to his legs.

He blinked a few more times, heart starting to race, panic building up in his body. The rusty metal door to the chamber was open—wide open. From the other side, he could hear the grunting and the howling of the undead.

A flash.

A memory crippling through his mind.

Severe pain in his right shoulder. Hayden leaning over him, Ally screaming as loud as he could, and ...

But no. That couldn't be a memory because it hadn't happened. Hayden had ... he'd strangled him. Knocked him out. And that's the last time he saw him. The last time he—

Another flash of a memory, this time so vivid that he could actually feel the pain crippling through his upper thigh.

Hear the sounds of tearing.

Slicing.

Feeling fear as he stared up at a blood-soaked Hayden, a demonic look in his eyes.

"Hel ... help." He tried to shout but his chest was tight. He'd read something once about heart problems being the cause of a bad chest. Heh. Heart problems were the least of anyone's concerns these days. No doctors left to keep everyone in check, no children to grow into doctors and start new research for a new generation.

Just death.

Death for everyone.

He reached to feel his chest again when he realised his right hand wasn't moving.

He turned to his right.

He didn't understand what he was looking at, at first. He had to blink to really wrap his head around it.

There was a gap where his right arm should be.

A gap where flesh dangled down from—flesh and veins spewing blood out onto the already blood-splattered tiles.

His right arm was missing.

He let out a pitiful yelp and swung around to look away, to

deny it. He hadn't lost his arm. That sick fucker hadn't taken his arm. He hadn't ...

And then he saw there was a space where his left arm should be, too.

More blood pooling out of the stump, tumbling to the floor.

He felt sickness grab hold of his gut and squeeze it. He tried to kick out, but doing so just hurt him even more ...

No. He can't have. He can't ...

Ally looked down and saw that the top portion of his legs had been stripped of flesh. Stripped so well that he could see the yellowing bone poking out from underneath the bloodbath.

And then in front of him on the tiles, he saw chunks of meat.

Chunks of meat leading towards the open door.

Chunks of meat cutting through the pool of blood, past the women he'd murdered, out into the dark ...

And just at the edge of the darkness, he saw movement.

He felt his vision slipping away. Felt himself growing dizzy—shock and blood loss. He knew this was it now. He knew there was no way out. He knew he was going to die in here.

He felt warm piss spreading around his blue jeans.

Tried to look away from the blood, from the flesh, but when he looked away, all he saw was the bodies of the women he'd killed, their vacant eyes all staring up at him and screaming YOU DID THIS YOU DID THIS YOU SICK FUCK.

"I ... I won't beg you," Ally said, as the footsteps got closer to the doorway. "I won't beg you, you fuck."

But when Hayden stepped inside the room, Ally's skin curdled.

It wasn't Hayden at all.

It was that raghead friend of Hayden's. Metal cuffs were wrapped around his torn wrists. He was looking right at Ally with hateful eyes.

Vacant eyes.

Blood covering his mouth.

And in one of his hands was Ally's leg, bite marks chewed out of it.

Ally's breathing grew shorter. His heart felt like it was going to burst through his chest. He shook and struggled against the chains around his chest. "Please!" he shouted. "Please!"

But that only made the raghead get closer.

Only made him drop the half-eaten leg and make a beeline for his hairy belly.

"I'm sorry!" Ally screamed, as he closed his eyes and struggled and waited and begged for mercy all at the same time. "I'm sorry for Clarice! I'm sorry for Clarice!"

He didn't feel any pain. He didn't hear any more footsteps. And he was convinced that it was over. He was dead. He'd died of shock yes shock and blood loss and all his pain was over and God would forgive him and—

He felt the teeth sink into his stomach.

Felt the raghead pull back on his skin and his muscle.

He screamed and cried and begged for it to be over quickly as his intestines spilled out of his body, as his bladder burst with the piercing intensity of teeth and whenever he passed out he woke up again with the pain, the pain, so bad, so intense, so agonising.

He screamed and apologised and begged for mercy.

It took another sixteen minutes of agony for Ally Harbridge to die of shock, blood loss and critical disemboweling.

And he felt every single millisecond.

FORTY

"I'm sorry for Clarice! I'm sorry for Clarice!"

Ally's voice rang in Hayden's ears as he stepped across the rain-soaked gravel of the Riversford Industrial Estate. Thunder crackled in the distance as rain continued to lash down on the ground. Water ran down his face, diluting the blood he was covered in. Over his shoulder he carried the rifle that had failed on him.

In his right hand, he held the knife he'd butchered Ally with.

"Your neck doesn't look good," Sarah said, as she walked beside Hayden. She was carrying the pistol that Hayden had left by the guard he'd killed outside. It didn't have loads of ammo left, but there would be enough to get by. She was dressed in a white T-shirt and grey jogging bottoms she'd found stashed at the side of the abattoir of butchered women. Her cheeks were cut and bruised. "Are you sure you're—"

"I'm fine," Hayden said. He looked ahead at the destroyed gates of Riversford. Looked at the crowd of the dead blocking their escape route, staggering in their direction. Truth was, he wasn't sure if he was fine. When Ally had stabbed the left side of his neck, he'd pierced his flesh and cut away a flap of skin.

Hayden was hardly choking, but he was under no illusions about needing stitches and medical attention.

But medical attention wasn't something anyone had the luxury of, not anymore.

"Watch out. On your left," Sarah said.

Hayden looked and saw two zombies power-walking towards him. A woman wearing a white dress and covered in blood, and a young boy who could be no older than eleven. Both of them coming towards them, tumbling over the rotting corpses of those who had fallen before them, coming in their direction.

Hayden pulled back the knife and cracked it right into the neck of the young boy while Sarah fired a bullet that pierced right through the woman's neck. As the zombie boy fell to the floor, Hayden noticed his lack of remorse. Noticed his lack of self-disgust. And in a way, he understood it. Desensitisation. He'd seen and done so many horrible things in the last week that the mere act of killing a zombie who was once a kid no longer fazed him in the way it used to do.

The way it *should* do.

What did that make him?

Where was the line between human and savage drawn?

"Should be able to skip past these and take the gates out," Sarah said, her fast walk turning into a jog. Rain fell from her greasy, soaked dark hair. "But we don't have long. Got another crowd heading our way. Now or never, Hayden."

Hayden looked around at the mass of bodies—those who had fallen, and those who were still undead—and he felt numbness crashing through him. He was surrounded by death. Death was everywhere. Death *always was* everywhere, sure, but now it was staring him in the face and reminding him of just how mortal he was.

Or in the case of the zombies, just how terrifying immortality could be.

He sliced the knife into the temple of another zombie that

threw itself at him, then stabbed another chubby one in its guts until its insides were mashed. He smashed the teeth of the ones that had fallen and whose necks hadn't been broken, cracked the necks where he could, fought through, battled through, edged closer to the gates, closer to freedom, Sarah by his side.

But what was freedom?

What was freedom now he didn't have Clarice in his life?

What was his life without his family? His family he'd grown so used to relying on; and then his little sister who he'd done his damnedest all his life to keep on the straight and narrow, to keep her spirits up, to be there for her.

What was life when he'd witnessed the death of the three people he cared most about in the world?

"Hayden, come on!" Sarah shouted as the wind howled around them. "We've gotta move. We've gotta get out of here before—"

And then she fell to the ground face first.

It took Hayden a moment to realise what had caused it.

There was a bald, topless zombie on the floor. It had been split into two right at the torso, but its arms were still flailing and its teeth were snapping as it moved in closer to Sarah's thigh.

Hayden pulled back his foot and swung it right into the zombie's face.

And then he pulled back again and again then kicked and stamped and kept on kicking and stamping until its head was just mush on the floor, until its teeth were caved in and its skull was cracked and eyes burst and still it kept on shaking its arms, waving them, trying to get a grip like a Daddy Long Legs' dismembered leg.

Sarah got back to her feet and Hayden was about to say something to her when she lifted her gun and pointed it at him.

He didn't know what to think at first. Didn't know what she was doing or why she was doing it.

She pulled the trigger.

A shot whizzed over Hayden's shoulder.

It was only when he heard the grunt that he turned around and saw there was a zombie right behind him—was being the operative word, now it lay on the floor with blood seeping out of its cracked head.

"Suppose that makes us even," Sarah said. "Now come on. We've got to get the hell out of here."

Hayden saw the fluid trickling out of the petrol canister Sarah had hit. Then he turned back and nodded.

They ran towards the gates. There was surprisingly little gunfire now, but then Hayden figured since Callum had been taken out and absent in the order-giving department, the little rats had gone wild and fled for their own lives. Because an illusion of order was all fair and well, but the moment that illusion was shattered, the second the gates were compromised and a horde marched through like a clown in a nice dream, everything good—everything perfect—all slipped away.

They reached the gates and Hayden looked back.

Bodies filled the parking area—still and moving. The lightning that cracked through the foundations of the sky lit up the silhouettes, as too did the moonlight. Hayden looked back at Riversford, looked at the chaos, and he couldn't help but feel a deep sadness that this place hadn't been the place it could've been. It could've been a place of real good. A shelter where the world really did restart itself without any of the psychopathic values Callum was instilling towards women.

A part of Hayden held out hope that there was a good place out there in the world somewhere. A place where people pulled together for the right reasons and not for the wrong.

But he'd seen what "good" was in this new world. "Good" was butchering a man for decapitating your sister. "Good" was torture, murder, no remorse.

If that was "good," then what hope did the world have?

"Hayden, we need to go," Sarah said. "I ... I don't know where, but we need to go."

Hayden took a deep breath of the rain-soaked air. He looked at the spot where his sister had fallen, where the life had seeped from her body in a painful matter of seconds.

He was about to turn around when he saw the movement inside the CityFast hangar.

"Do you see that?" Hayden asked.

Sarah looked out of the gates, paced back and forth. "Hayden, we need to—"

He lifted a finger. Pointed at that window on the second floor. "I ... I think there's somebody in there."

"They're just the dead. And even if there is someone, there's nothing we can do for them now."

But then, in the next flash of lightning, Hayden saw exactly what was through the window.

A black woman with a little girl of about ten beside her.

Both standing naked by that window and staring out with fear on their faces.

The little girl was holding a sign up, and it was in the next flash of lightning that Hayden saw the words.

Five of us. We're prisoners and trapped. Please someone please help.

FORTY-ONE

For all the destruction and chaos surrounding Hayden, it was that little girl holding up the sign inside the hangar window and begging for help that clung on to Hayden's attention.

"Hayden, there's nothing we can do," Sarah said. Rain lashed down from the dark, thunderous sky in droves. In the grounds of the Riversford Industrial Estate, the dead marched in Hayden and Sarah's direction. There was a clear route out for them both. They could turn around and run—run off into the night, into the darkness, find another place to shelter.

But those people in the window.

The woman and her daughter. The fear on their faces.

He couldn't just leave them behind. Not after all he'd already lost.

He started to walk back through the gates when he felt Sarah pull him back. It stung the side of his neck, which still leaked with blood from Ally's stabbing.

"Hayden, you can't save everyone. You might think you can but you can't."

But saving everyone wasn't Hayden's concern.

Saving *someone* was.

Because he'd lost too many people. Lost far too many people. And sure, he'd gone back and he'd got Sarah free of the chains before Ally had a chance to kill her. But she wasn't enough. One person wasn't enough. It was like being undercharged for fish and chips and only repaying the cost of the chips through honesty—a half-job.

"I'm going in there and I'm going to get them out of here," Hayden said.

He pulled away from Sarah yet again and made his way back onto the waterlogged tarmac of the industrial estate.

"But how will you—"

"I'll find a way," Hayden said. "I have to find a way. We can't just start giving up on people, otherwise what humanity do we have? We're supposed to help each other. Look out for each other, no matter what. But if we just leave these people to die, what makes us so different from the Riversford people?"

"We're completely different to the Riversford people."

"Are we?" Hayden asked. He raised his eyebrows, felt blood crusted in his frown lines. "I'm going. I'm going because it's something I have to do. You get started. Get running away from this place. I'll find you. We'll find you."

Hayden turned and continued his walk, the knife tightly wrapped between his fingers. He could see a few zombies drifting his way from the left. And then a few more over by the hangar door, congregating underneath the woman and the child who were desperate, begging for help.

"Oh screw it. Screw it."

Hayden looked over his shoulder and saw Sarah catching up with him.

"I always bloody end up following you one way or other. You're like the frigging Pied Piper or something. If this kills me, just sleep soundly in the knowledge that I *will* hold it against you."

Hayden lifted the knife and stabbed it through the sinewy neck of an oncoming zombie. "You'll be way too dead to hold anything against me."

The pair of them ran towards the doors of the hangar. Hayden kicked back a few zombies, but most of the time he tried to dodge them. But their dead mass was growing more claustrophobic, more suffocating. And as the clouds moved across the moon and the lightning eased, avoiding them became progressively difficult.

He didn't want to look back at the pile of unfinished zombies he'd left lying in his wake. He knew there was still a part two to this mission: getting the hell out of here when they'd rescued the family.

One step at a time, perhaps.

Optimistic naivety, more likely.

A white-haired zombie clutched at Hayden's ankles as he passed. Long hair, male, wearing a black biker jacket. Rotting teeth lined his gums. His body split in two at the hips, the bottom half dangling on by a few stringy threads of flesh and skin.

Hayden didn't feel any remorse. He didn't even have to think about swinging the knife across its mouth, then crouching down and cracking its neck in his hands. But when he stood he saw another zombie coming his way—a skinny girl with auburn hair, her teeth so cracked through grinding that they were as sharp as a vampire's.

Sarah lifted her gun and fired at the zombie but no sound came out. She looked at the gun, tried to fire again but still to no sound. "It's jammed. It's frigging jammed—"

And then another zombie rose from the darkness and grabbed her ankle.

Dragged her to the ground.

Hayden let go of the biker's neck and reached for his knife.

And then he felt something smack into his left side and knock him to the ground.

The knife fell from his hand.

Sarah shouted in pain.

FORTY-TWO

Sarah's scream made Hayden's skin prick up with goose pimples.

He struggled around on the soaking wet floor, the dampness spreading through his clothes and reminding him just how damned cold it really was. The zombie kept on clutching onto his left side. He couldn't see it in the darkness, but he could hear its throaty drawl, smell its rotting body pressing him further and further down.

Teeth snapping.

Moving closer to the side of his body.

Towards his stomach ...

And then he saw Sarah. Saw the two zombies on top of her. Saw her shaking and struggling as she fought hand to hand with the zombies, but they too were closing in on her. As the rain lashed down, the mass of zombies approached. This was getting worse before it could get better.

No. Hayden couldn't allow that. He couldn't let somebody else die. He couldn't lose another person. Another friend.

So he swung his fist around and cracked his hand into the zombie's face. He felt the thing's snapping teeth, felt his knuckles crack against them, milliseconds from closing in on his hand and biting him.

But he had no other choice. No other way.

He struggled and swung again. Punched the zombie in the face and the neck repeatedly until it backed off some, and then kept on punching as it backed off, still holding on to his left arm, snarling and spewing cold blood and raw innards out of its disfigured face.

He gained some ground and heard Sarah shout again. He didn't even want to look. He didn't want to see her being bitten because he didn't want to accept failure, not again.

So he kept on punching at the zombie. Kept on punching until its face was bloodied and distorted and Hayden's knuckles stung and ached like mad.

He saw the other zombies coming. Tons of them wandering through the cold, damp darkness of the Riversford Industrial Estate. They'd be on him in seconds. On Sarah in seconds. They'd never get out of here. They'd never save the woman and her kid from the room.

They'd die here. Each one of them would die here. More names to add to the world's ever-growing list of newly deceased.

He saw the zombie's mouth closing in on his arm as it kept gripping on.

He felt the weight on his back. The weight of the rifle that wasn't working. No time to fix it now. No time to try to figure out what the hell was wrong with it.

But he reached over onto his back.

Gripped the front of it.

The zombie's teeth descended on Hayden's arm.

Hayden held his breath and swung the rifle right into the zombie's skull.

He heard a crack, like an Easter egg splitting.

And then he swung the rifle again and again at the zombie's neck until he heard another crack, more splitting.

And then the zombie tumbled to the floor, shook and twitched like a seizure victim.

Hayden wanted to make sure it was definitely dead. He wanted to deal with the larger crowd swarming this way.

But Sarah ...

He turned around and readied to swing the gun at the zombies standing over her.

Nobody was taking her. Nobody was taking anyone else away from him.

But what he saw wasn't exactly what he expected.

Sarah was standing in front of Hayden. Her white T-shirt was covered in blood and dirt. The zombies that had been crawling over her were on the ground beside her, holes in the sides of their heads.

It took Hayden a few seconds to realise there was someone standing behind Sarah.

"You left me to die, you fucker. You left me to die."

The chubby, balding guy who'd been tied up with Hayden and Manish.

And he was holding a sharp-edged pole to Sarah's exposed neck.

FORTY-THREE

"Put the pole down. Nobody has to get hurt here."

The chubby guy with the sharp, bloodied pole to Sarah's neck peered at Hayden with hateful eyes, which illuminated in the dim glow of rain-battered moonlight. "You left me to die, you fuck. You left me to die and—and look what went and happened 'cause you left me to die."

Hayden didn't understand what the chubby guy was referring to at first. And then he saw the mark on his right arm. The bite marks, deep into his flesh, blood dripping down from them. He was shaking, sweating, like he was angry at the world and was taking his anger out on anyone, anything he could.

"Please. Just put the weapon down and we can figure this out—"

"Figure this out?" the chubby guy shouted. He smiled a little, sweat and rain pouring down his head. "I've been bit. All thanks to you I've been bit. You fuck. You fuck."

Hayden glanced to the left. The large crowd of zombies was approaching and getting quicker as it did. There was absolutely no way they were escaping through the main gates now. There was only one way to go, and that was inside.

Inside to whatever lay ahead.

"We can go inside and we can get safe. We can ... we can—"

"There is no fuckin' safety here," the chubby man said. Hayden swore he was sobbing, swore he saw tears rolling out of his hopeless, pitiful eyes. "No fuckin' safety for me or—or my wife or kids. No safety for anyone here."

Hayden glanced to the left again. The zombies were approaching fast. He looked back and saw Sarah nodding at him; nodding at him to go on, to get out of here, to leave her behind.

And a part of Hayden was tempted. A part of Hayden that still remained from his days of cowardice considered turning around and running.

But no. He'd run away too many times in his life already. And he'd left Sarah behind before, so never again.

She'd come with him. She'd put everything on the line to help rescue the innocents from the hangar. He couldn't just give up on her.

"Please," Hayden said, his voice drowned out by the crackling of thunder from above. "I'm begging you not to do this. And I'm sorry for leaving you behind. But we can go inside. We can go inside and put all of this behind us and focus on the next step. Because we need to focus on the next step."

The chubby guy's eyes narrowed. More zombies approached from behind him, lit up in the moonlight. He tightened his grip around Sarah's neck. "You ... you'll just kill me. You'll just throw me away to be like them."

Hayden shook his head. His heart pounded as the footsteps of the surrounding zombies echoed closer. "I won't," he shouted. "I won't leave you behind. We need to go inside. We need to move. Now!"

The chubby guy glanced over his shoulder at the zombies that were just five, four metres away.

And then he looked back at Hayden, jaw shaking, eyes wide. He nodded. "Thank you. Thank you."

He lowered the pipe from Sarah's neck and Sarah pulled herself free.

Hayden nodded back at the chubby guy. But in a way he felt a sadness. A sadness about the bite in his arm. A sadness about what that meant.

He turned and started jogging in the direction of the hangar door.

Reached down and picked up his fallen knife then carried on running, the zombies nipping at their heels.

And when they reached the concrete steps he stopped.

Turned around.

"I'm sorry," he said. "I hope you understand."

The chubby guy's eyes narrowed. "Understand what—"

Hayden stabbed him in the neck.

He yanked the knife out of his flabby neck and turned around before he had the chance to see the chubby guy glug, see him fall over in shock and crack his head on the concrete, sending him into a merciful unconsciousness as the crowd of zombies sunk their teeth into his blubber, tore the meat from his bones, feasted.

Sarah looked at Hayden with horror as Hayden opened the door. "Come on," he said.

Her eyes narrowed. She looked back at the chubby guy being torn into pieces. "You ... you ..."

"He was bitten. I did what I had to do. Now get inside."

Sarah walked slowly past Hayden, like she was stuck in some kind of trance.

Hayden listened to the sounds of tearing flesh, but he didn't look back.

He only looked forward. That's all he could do right now.

All anyone could do.

FORTY-FOUR

They moved quickly and silently down the darkened corridor and towards the room that the family were penned into.

Hayden led the way and Sarah followed closely behind. At the doors, the handles of which they'd wedged a metal pipe between, the sound of gasping, tearing, of footsteps approaching followed their every move. The knowledge that those doors wouldn't hold forever—that eventually, this building would be compromised and the entire Riversford Industrial Estate would be lost—gnawed at Hayden's sanity like a fox at a trapped leg.

"Was it the third floor they were on?" Sarah asked, breaking the deafening silence.

Hayden looked around the empty CityFast hangar. It looked so intact. So ... safe and secure. It was hard to believe that an army of zombies was on the verge of taking this place—no need for it, but they flowed into empty spaces like water. "Second. Second, I think."

Sarah slowed her run and panted. She put her hands on her hips and looked around. "There might still be time to get away," she said. "We ... we can still turn around and—"

"Stairs are over there," Hayden said, pointing just past Sarah and to the staircase leading up to the upper floors of the hangar.

Sarah looked as if she was about to say something in objection, then decided against it. And that's because she must've seen it. Must've seen the look on Hayden's face—the determination. Nothing was stopping him from reaching those innocent people in that room. Nothing was stopping him, even if it meant self-sacrifice.

She followed him as he reached the bottom steps of the hangar. He looked up. Kept the knife tightly between his fingers. He'd lost track of how much his pierced neck was stinging, how dizzy his head was and how dry his throat was growing. And it had to stay that way. He couldn't think about himself, not until he saved these people.

He wasn't letting anyone else innocent die.

But then again, who even was innocent anymore? And what was it to *be* innocent?

He powered up the staircase. He had to be ready for anyone who'd stuck behind of the Riversford group to leap out, attack him. Some of them had to have stayed back. Most of them would have fled, but they couldn't all be gone.

"We have to watch out," Sarah called. "We have to think about —about what we're going to say."

"There's nothing to say," Hayden said, reaching the top of the staircase. He kept his eyes ahead. "This place is lost. Those people need help getting out of here. We—"

His voice was interrupted by an echoing thump against the main door of the hangar. He swung around, and so too did Sarah. Then she looked back at him, her face a new shade of pale. "They're coming. We have to hurry. We have to do whatever the hell it is we've got to do and then we've got to get the hell out of here."

Hayden heard another thump at the door.

Sarah was right. They didn't have much time.

He swung over and poked his head around the sides of the staircase exits. On the left: nothing but a desk similar to the one Callum used to sit at, his murderous drawings in the top drawer.

On the left ... a door.

The door was closed, but Hayden knew there was somebody inside. He could see the shadows of feet moving around in there. And he couldn't hear any growling or gasping—just the faintest of whispers.

His heart picked up in pace. He turned and looked at Sarah, then nodded.

This was the room. This was the place where the survivors were. This was—

Another crack against the main door of the hangar. A crack that sent shivers up Hayden's arms. Rain and wind battered against the foundations of the building, and the urgency of the situation welled up inside Hayden. They had to get in here and they had to get out.

They had to be quick.

He walked slowly towards the door and he heard another whisper ahead of him. He thought about what to say. The people on the other side of this door could be armed, ready to strike. He had to put them at ease. He had to make his presence known without scaring them.

"It's ... it's Hayden." He felt stupid for saying that straight away. "I ... I was a prisoner here. I'm one of the ..." He was going to say "one of the good guys," but he wasn't too sure even he believed that anymore. "I saw your sign. And I'm here to help you out."

Nothing but silence at the other side of the door. But there was a feeling. Hayden couldn't describe it any other way than a *feeling* of someone being there; knowledge of a presence.

He waited for a response. Waited for a sound. But beyond the wind, the rain, the snarling of the zombies gathered in the grounds outside, there was nothing.

Hayden looked back at Sarah, who rubbed her arms and kept on glancing at the stairs they'd headed up. And then he turned back to the door. Grabbed the handle. "I'm going to come inside. Just ... please. I'm not going to hurt you. I... I lost someone here too. We all lost someone here. I'm going to come inside. Right now. Please."

He hesitated for a few seconds. Jumped when a blast of thunder crackled overhead.

And then he gripped tighter hold of the handle.

Held his breath.

Lowered it.

When he pushed the door open, the first thing that startled him were the eyes.

There were lots of them. Eyes, all looking at him, all wide and focused and bloodshot.

The eyes of five, six, seven people.

Men. Women. Children.

And then he saw the eyes of the little girl by the window, her mum's arm around her shoulder. He saw her eyes and he just knew, right away.

He knew she was Newbie's daughter. She didn't have to say a thing. He just knew.

The people looked on, scared, hesitant. Two of them were men dressed in the same green slacks that Ally and the other CityFast goons wore. But they didn't look threatening. They looked terrified. Holed up in here and at the end of their tether; the end of the line.

Hayden cleared his throat and stepped a little further into the darkened room.

"I'm ... I'm Hayden. This is Sarah. We're going to get out of here. All of us. We're going to—"

Hayden didn't finish what he wanted to say.

He heard the bang against the main door of the hangar.

He heard something snap and then the sound of metal echoing against the floor.

And then, he heard the echoing gasp of zombies stagger inside the building.

FORTY-FIVE

"We need to get the hell out of here. Quick!"

Hayden didn't have time for pleasantries with the new group. That time would come—hopefully, anyway.

But that hope was wearing thin as the zombies gathered inside the hangar, swarmed through the bottom floor, all seeking their next meal, all looking out for a grand prize that they weren't even conscious to appreciate.

"Hayden, seriously!" Sarah said, to-ing and fro-ing along the corridor outside the room. "They're filling up the downstairs hall. They'll be up here in no time. We need to make a fucking break for it."

Hayden turned and looked at the group. Two men in CityFast outfits with terrified faces, one of them clutching a pistol with his life. The black woman and the ten-year-old girl who had to be Newbie's daughter. What must be a couple in their early forties holding hands with one another, their young boy stuck between them, the bruises on his face nothing compared to the mental scars this place would leave in his mind.

"All of us need to leave here right this second. Zombies are filling up the downstairs hall. We need to—"

"It's no fucking use," Sarah said. She ran back into the room and slammed the door, surrounding everyone in darkness. Hayden thought he could hear her pounding heartbeat from here. "They ... they're coming up the stairs. They saw me. They're coming."

The little boy started to cry. His mum whispered fearful words of reassurance to him. The men in the CityFast gear cursed. Newbie's ex-wife and daughter just stood by the window and stared, the calmest and most composed of the entire group.

Hayden looked Newbie's wife in the eye and at that moment in time, as the sound of the zombies crawling up the stairs, tripping and tumbling over one another, got gradually closer, he had no idea how they were going to get out of this situation. They were trapped. Nine of them trapped together in a tiny room. A feast for the zombies.

Because the zombies would find them. They'd sniff them out like they always did. And it didn't matter how hard the group fought, those kinds of numbers couldn't be dealt with by hand. They could hold them off. Maybe even stay on their feet for five or ten or fifteen minutes, fighting and fighting.

But eventually one of them would slip. One of them would fall.

That would be the start of the end.

The thunder crackled and lightning lit the room up in a blue, nightmarish hue. The little boy cried again, his parents reassured and calmed him again, but Hayden could hear the acknowledging fear in their voices, too.

He could hear the change in the snarls of the zombies. He could hear the way they echoed differently—a sure sign that they were up the stairs, on their level.

And he wanted to do something. He wanted to go out there and fight. He wanted to try to make a break for it.

But all he could do was stand still.

Count down the minutes.

Count down the seconds.

Life was ending.

He joined the collective silence of the room and his vision grew dreamy as he stared out into the dark. The grounds were filled with zombies. Some of them had branched off into the City Link building, others were still outside. He saw the bodies on the ground. The fallen bodies of men, women. Some of them good people, some of them bad people, but all of them people.

And then his mind's eye wandered to the spot where Clarice had fallen. Where just metres away, he'd stood and he'd watched Ally slice her head from her body. He remembered the feeling that came over him then, as the footsteps of the zombies got closer to the room door. He remembered that stunned, dreamlike feeling of being frozen in time, prisoner to his emotions.

He felt it again.

Only this time he couldn't find the key out.

He felt a hand on his arm. Looked to his left and saw Sarah by his side. She looked into his eyes, tears in the crystal blue of hers, and she attempted a smile but it was weak and pointless. It was terrifying.

It was that look he'd imagined so many times since the world ended.

The look of knowledge. Of, "this is it, we're going to die and there's nothing we can do about it."

But the thing that terrified Hayden most was that he knew he was looking at Sarah in the same way.

He looked around at all these people and he felt so sad for them. Newbie's ex-wife and daughter. The entire reason they'd headed to Warrington in the first place. At least they'd made it this far. That was something, wasn't it? This entire journey wasn't all for ...

And then he remembered something.

Sarah pointing her gun at the zombie outside.

The bullet firing past the zombie, puncturing the petrol canisters.

Petrol pouring to the ground and bathing the zombies in a waterfall of flammable fluid.

"I ... I think I've got something."

Hayden rushed over to the window. He could hear people asking him what he was talking about, hear confusion and panic and puzzlement.

He looked out of the window and at the massive green canister, other canisters of petrol packed on top of them, petrol splashing out of the pierced one and hitting the ground below.

"Hayden, what's—"

"A lighter," Hayden said. "Does anyone in here have a lighter?"

He looked around. Looked at the two CityFast men and Newbie's ex-wife and the couple in their forties.

Zombie footsteps getting closer.

Mangled hands scraping against the corridor walls.

"A lighter," Hayden said sterner. "Does anyone have—"

"Yes. Yes." The muscular man in a CityFast uniform held out a gold lighter to Hayden with his shaking hand.

Hayden reached down and snatched it away.

"I—I don't think that's gonna hold 'em off," the muscular man said. "They ain't much scared of the flames."

"I need your gun, too," Hayden said.

He looked at the other CityFast guy. Looked at the pistol clutched in his hand.

"I—I need this. Only got six bullets. Need to use 'em when we absolutely need to."

"We absolutely need to," Hayden said.

He reached down and grabbed the cold metal of the gun. He looked the CityFast man in the eyes.

"You need to trust me. It's the only chance we have here. Please."

The CityFast man loosened his grip on the gun.

Hayden edged it away.

He walked over to the window and with the butt of the gun he smashed it open.

He heard the group curse and shout out behind him. Heard them telling him to "ssh!"

Heard a deathly silence.

And then a zombie thumping itself against the door.

He pushed away some of the loose shards of glass from the side of the window and leaned out into the cold windy night. He heard another bang at the door, heard more shrieks and cries, but he kept his focus, kept his mind set on the only thing he could think to do.

It was suicide. But sometimes people survived suicide attempts.

Nobody survived the zombies.

He pointed the gun at the pile of green petrol canisters and he fired.

Six.

Five.

Four.

Another bang at the door.

Someone by his side telling him they needed the ammo, screaming at him they needed to get the hell out of here or at least try to defend the place and—Oh God they're coming in I can see them I can see them.

He fired again.

Two shots left.

One shot left.

And then he passed the gun back to the CityFast guy as the wood of the door caved in, as the zombies clawed their way inside the room, as pandemonium erupted.

He looked at the petrol water falling out of the canisters and he rolled back the lighter.

He hoped to God his video game logic had got this right.

He pulled his arm back.

Kept the lighter burning.

And then he threw.

The lighter moved through the air in slow motion. And one second it was there and then it was gone, completely gone, and as the gasps of the zombies echoed out just a few metres behind him, Hayden knew he'd lost. He'd fucked it up. He'd screwed everything up.

And then in the darkness there was light.

FORTY-SIX

The moment the flames went up was the moment Hayden knew that beauty still existed in this morally desolate world.

It happened fast. Not in a slo-mo montage like in a clichéd movie or anything like that. It happened so quickly that he didn't even have time to process it.

One moment, there was nothing but darkness.

The next moment, flames.

Flames engulfed the petrol canisters. They burned through the petrol that waterfalled out of those canisters, hit the ground and then everything erupted. It happened so fast. Quicker than Hayden could comprehend.

Dark, then light.

Flames zipped across the entire Riversford grounds and set the place alight.

Set the zombies alight.

The smell of hundreds of burning bodies filled the air, and yet it was the most beautiful thing Hayden had ever seen.

He would have waited. Waited and watched all night as the flames burned away the remnants of the zombies, as the light engulfed more of the petrol canisters and sparked more explosions. He could've stood there in the heat and he could've watched the badness burn away in the beautifully white-hot light.

But he heard the door to the room splitting away, heard the little boy scream, and he knew he couldn't stand around.

He gripped tight hold of the knife and he turned to face the zombies stepping inside the room. There were fewer of them than he'd imagined. They lit up in the orange glow of their burning peers outside.

"Make sure you're armed!" Hayden shouted as the zombies piled inside the room. "Aim for the neck!"

And then he lifted the knife and he held his breath and ran at the zombies.

When he ran into them and swung at the flesh on their necks and skulls and wherever he could manage, he didn't feel fear. Instead, he just kept his sister in mind. Kept Newbie, Manish, Frank, Usman—all the people he'd lost, he kept them in mind.

His parents.

He kept his parents in mind as he rammed the sharp edge of the blade into the back of the neck of a short, dark-haired zombie.

He felt them encouraging him as he stabbed an ageing bald man through his neck, the metallic stench of cold blood mixing with the char grilled meat outside. He felt them encouraging him to fight on, as Sarah fought, as the two CityFast men fought, as everyone fought.

He didn't feel fear.

He just felt different.

He didn't feel any kind of emotion when one of the CityFast men—the one who'd given Hayden the lighter— fell and a zombie sunk its teeth into his ankle.

He just kept on fighting, kept focused on the six, five zombies that were in front of him, and when he had the chance he sliced the back of the neck of the zombie that had bitten the CityFast man, and then he rammed the blade into the head of the CityFast man despite his begging, despite his protestations.

He didn't feel fear. He didn't feel sadness.

Just different.

Changed.

He was doing what he had to do to survive. He understood that now.

The group kept on fighting until there were just two left, then one left, and then nothing but a gap between the door and the staircase.

And then the eight of them that remained ran. They ran out of the room, away from the orange glow, away from the sounds of melting skin outside.

But they didn't run down the staircase.

They ran past the staircase and then up another set of stairs. And when they reached the floor where Callum's office was, they ran over to the scaffolding and looked down. It wasn't burning down there. Not yet. It would be soon, but not yet. Everything would be burning soon.

They climbed down the scaffolding, all of them, and then they climbed over the fence that Hayden had sneaked back into Riversford via. They fought off more zombies. Snapped their necks. Sliced their heads. But the bulk of them were burning. Burning to a crisp. They crumbled away under a tap of the knife.

They climbed over the fence and dropped to the other side.

They ran. Ran and fought and ran some more as the clouds began to part and bright moonlight replaced the murky, thundery gaze.

And after they'd run for God knows how long they looked back, all of them, at Riversford. Looked at the flames as they spread across the grounds. Looked at the side of the hangar as it caught fire, as the flames reached the scaffolding and brought it down, as the windows inside the hangar started to crack.

All eight of the survivors stood and watched the flames like a family around a campfire on a cold winter's day, and for a moment, everything was okay. Everything in the world was fine.

And tomorrow, it wouldn't be. In five minutes, it might not be. There'd be some other crowd of zombies or some other humans with bad intentions that would flock this way.

But right now, right here in this moment of time, everything was fine.

Despite everything Hayden had done, everything he'd lost, everything was fine.

He watched the smoke rise from Riversford and he felt like he was home.

FORTY-SEVEN

"All clear?"

"All clear."

Hayden twiddled a daffodil shoot in his left finger and yanked the knife out of the side of the head of the charred zombie. Its body had set on fire several hours ago, in the darkness of night, but the smell of burning was still strong in the morning air. Now and then, as Hayden and the other seven survivors cleared out the grounds of Riversford, Hayden swore he heard flames crackling or screams radiating out, but whenever he looked up all he saw was the ashen remains of the undead, burned out to a crisp and left to wriggle morbidly in the low winter sun.

Sarah stepped up beside Hayden. Her hands were covered with black marks, the remnants of the burned bodies they'd obliterated. "Pity they aren't all burned to a crisp. Might make our job a little easier."

Hayden nodded in agreement. Sarah had a point. The zombies just crumbled to pieces when they'd been burned—they had no problem breaking their necks. And that's what they'd spent the morning doing. Ever since the sun rose, ever since the flames died down, they'd been clearing this place out.

Because there was something with this place. Aspects of it that were worth holding onto.

"Are you sure about staying here?" Sarah asked, catching Hayden in his thoughts.

Hayden looked around the grounds. The major issue was the fallen fence. "We can use wood from the forest to build some new fences. Make it safer and stronger than it ever was before. And we can make ourselves scarcer than the CityFast group. We can work together. When we see zombie approaching, we make damned sure we have a proper plan in order—even if that means a legitimate evacuation plan."

Sarah nodded. "The main hangar. It's all burned out."

"There's three other hangars in this vicinity. More than that at the other side of the fences. The CityFast group chose this place for a reason—it has solid foundations. It's secure. And Riversford's a big place. If we need to move on to another hangar, we can do."

"And what about this lot?" Sarah asked. She pointed at the six people who had joined them, the six people they'd rescued from the CityFast room last night. Gary, the CityFast employee, currently walking around with a spade and smashing the skulls of any zombies that remained undead. Matt and Karen and their little boy, Tim, who sat at the side with their arms around one another, teeth chattering in the cold. And then there was Martha. Newbie's ex-wife.

Amy. Newbie's daughter. The whole damned reason Newbie had come to Warrington in the first place.

"I think they're good people," Hayden said.

"You don't sound certain."

"I'm not. I can't be certain. None of us can be certain about anybody anymore. Not even me about you or you about me."

He side-glanced at Sarah and saw her lower her head to look at the ash and debris covered floor. Somewhere overhead, crows cawed. "Are you going to tell them?"

"Tell them what? What I just told—"

"About Newbie. Are you going to tell Martha and ... and Amy about what happened to Newbie?"

Hayden looked at Martha and Amy. There was a smile on Amy's face. An actual smile. Martha caught Hayden looking and lifted a hand, and Hayden nodded back.

"In time. They deserve to know. Just ... just not now."

"How can you be the decider of when the right time is?"

"I can't," Hayden said. He lifted his knife and stuck it into the neck of another zombie on the ground in front. Its top half had been severed from the bottom, and its eyes had withered away in the heat. The skin and flesh was as easy as paper to tear, and it went silent within a second of contact with the knife. "I'm just trying my best here. Trying my best to keep in control of things. Because ... because we all need to be in control. But right now, more than anything, we need a little hope. We all need a little hope."

Hayden walked over to the spot where Clarice's head had been severed from her neck. He crouched down on the spot that he was convinced she'd fallen, and he laid down the dandelion shoot on top of the ashes.

Sarah swallowed a lump in her throat. She wiped her eyes and cleared her throat. "Why now more than anything?"

Hayden stared at the dandelion shoot. He saw Clarice's smiling face. He saw her with Mum and Dad and Annabelle. He saw them all looking down on him, all smiling and laughing, all so proud of their boy for making it so far.

And then he looked up at the grounds. He looked up at the walls, at the hangars. Some of this place burned, sure, but nothing that couldn't be repaired, nothing that couldn't be patched up and maintained.

Then he saw the people. The six people Sarah and he had saved. Should've been seven—should've been more than that—

but they'd saved these six from the jaws of death and they'd given them another chance. They'd given them another day.

They'd given them hope.

"We need it now more than anything because we're about to start."

Sarah's eyes narrowed. "Start what?"

Hayden turned away from the daffodil and smiled.

"Living again."

WANT MORE INFECTION Z?

The third book in the Infection Z series is now available.

If you want to be notified when Ryan Casey's next novel is released (and receive a free book from his Dead Days post apocalyptic series), please sign up for the mailing list by going to: http://ryancaseybooks.com/fanclub Your email address will never be shared and you can unsubscribe at any time.

Word-of-mouth and reviews are crucial to any author's success. If you enjoyed this book, please leave a review. Even just a couple of lines sharing your thoughts on the story would be a fantastic help for other readers.

For a full up to date list of all the author's books, head over to this link: http://ryancaseybooks.com/books